THE SHOWDOWN

Mr. Pinkerton felt uneasy breaking into a chap's apartment—even though the chap was a killer, a thief and a thorough cad. He was glad the door opened effortlessly at the first push.

Inspector Bull walked boldly in with drawn gun; Mr. Pinkerton hovered behind. They were taking the man by surprise; he sat with his back to the door, the stolen jewels on a table beside him. "Hands up, you blackguard!" yelled Inspector Bull, "We've caught you red-handed!"

There was no reply, which wasn't so strange, thought Mr. Pinkerton. After all, the chap was rather dead.

TWO AGAINST SCOTLAND YARD

■ BY DAVID FROME

WILDSIDE PRESS

CHAPTER ONE

On the evening of Wednesday, February 25th, 1931, a man stood in the shadow of the entrance to the grounds of a large house on the Colnbrook Road, about a quarter of a mile from the London end of the by-pass. Beside him, turned towards town, was a motorcycle. Its engine was running quietly, but the rider made no move towards leaving. Several times he glanced over his shoulder at the white "For Sale" placards on the gate posts, or looked nervously at the watch on his wrist. Now and then his hand stole to the packet of cigarettes in his coat pocket, but he changed his mind each time.

The illuminated hands of his watch showed exactly nine-twenty-two o'clock when he heard the purr of a motor car coming from his right. He stepped into the middle of the road. As the big Daimler came into view he held up his hand. The car stopped a few feet from him. The chauffeur lowered the window, leaned out to see what was wanted, and found himself staring into the cold steel circle of a revolver muzzle. Another was pointed steadily at the two people in the back of the car.

"Get out," said the man. "Keep your hands up."

The chauffeur got out, holding his hands over his head.

"Stand over there."

The chauffeur stepped promptly over to the side of the road.

"Now you get out and put that satchel on the ground."

The heavily built man, grey-haired, in evening clothes, moved clumsily towards the door of the car. The woman with him started to follow.

"You stay where you are."

The man took one step back from the car, his revolvers pointing steadily at the two men. The elderly man still held the small black satchel in his hands.

"Put that down, or I'll shoot you," the man said calmly.

"Give it to him, for God's sake, George!" the woman cried.

As the man stooped to put the satchel down her hand moved stealthily to the side pocket of the car. Without moving her shoulders she whipped a small automatic out of it and brought it to a level with her knees. As the bandit with a sharp movement of his foot brought the satchel near him she fired through the open door and sank back into the cushions.

Instantly two shots rang out, so close to hers that the reports could almost have been one drawn-out sound rather than three. The heavy man in evening clothes pitched forward without a word. There was the rush of feet, the roar of an engine, and the cyclist disappeared in the darkness towards London.

The chauffeur ducked forward, his face grey in the glare of the headlights. He bent over his employer. The woman, white and shaking, stumbled out of the car.

"What made you shoot, madam?" the chauffeur asked in a hushed voice. "You nearly caught me."

The woman stared at him in terror.

"The diamonds!" she gasped.

"Lord! did he have diamonds with him?" The chauffeur whistled, and glanced about.

"I'd better go for a constable," he said after a moment's thought.

"No. I can't stay here alone with him. I'll go."

"Here comes somebody now, madam."

A man came running awkwardly towards them along the road.

"Hi there," the chauffeur said. "There's a man dead. Run and get the police, will you?"

The man gave a long stare at the scene. "Right you are," he said. "I'll get my push-bike." He turned and ran back into the darkness.

The woman sank to the running board and stared blindly at the prostrate figure on the ground. She scarcely noticed the small crowd of sleepy villagers that had gathered. They stood whispering at a respectful distance, staring at the great car, the woman in the ermine cloak, and the figure lying motionless on the ground. The chauffeur moved back and forth trying to light a cigarette. His hands shook and he dropped the match.

The woman suddenly got up and started pacing the road. "Oh, why don't they hurry?" she cried in an agony of despair.

" 'Obbs is off on 'is push-bike, miss," one of the bystanders volunteered. " 'E cahn't make it short of five minutes."

"More like ten, as I'd say," said another. There was a muttered altercation.

It was a good ten minutes before a murmur broke from the little knot of watchers.

"Ay, there 'e is, and Jock Gibney with him."

The young constable got off his bicycle and propped it against the hedge on the other side of the road. The woman came quickly forward to meet him.

"My husband's been robbed and killed," she said quickly. "Heaven knows how far the man has got already."

The constable was more used to arresting cyclists without lights than comforting London ladies in ermine wraps. He cleared his throat and looked about in some embarrassment. Then he set about his work with dogged determination.

"Just tell me what happened, madam," he said, "and I'll get at it as quick as I can."

"We were held up right here by a man on a motorcycle. He made my husband give him a satchel we had. I thought I could frighten him. I shot at him and he shot my husband. Oh, it's all my fault!"

She began to sob convulsively.

"It won't help none to let yourself get in a state, ma'am," the constable said stolidly. He knelt down over the dead man and flashed his lamp into his face.

"He was your husband?"

"Yes."

"Could you describe the man? He was on a motorcycle?"

She nodded.

"You didn't see the number?"

She shook her head. The constable turned to the chauffeur. "I didn't see it," he said. "He must have had the plates covered. I looked."

The constable scratched his head, then brightened as there was another murmur from the group of bystanders.

"That'll be the sergeant," he said cheerfully.

The circle opened; a small car drove up and the division sergeant stepped out.

"What's up?" he said. When the constable had given the meagre details he knelt over the silent figure.

He straightened up after a short examination.

"Shot twice," he said laconically. "Once through the heart. Instantaneous death. What was the man like?"

Neither the woman nor the chauffeur could give anything but a vague description. The murderer had worn a cyclist's leather cap and large goggles, with a black mask over the lower part of his face. He was taller than the dead man but slenderer, the chauffeur thought; the woman thought he was the same height.

The sergeant shrugged his shoulders. "Just like everybody else riding a motorcycle, and he's been gone fifteen minutes. Gibney, you go back with the lady and the driver to the sta-

7

tion. Drive back in their car. Put in a call to Scotland Yard and tell them exactly what's happened. Tell them the motorcycle left here at 9.24 or 9.25, headed towards town."

He turned to the woman.

"I'll have to ask you to go back to Colnbrook for a bit, madam. If there's anybody you'd like to have come, the constable will give them a ring."

She shook her head, and taking a last agonised look at the figure on the ground got into the car. The chauffeur took his place. The young constable got in beside him, and they drove off slowly into the little village.

At the tiny police station the constable reported the night's event to Scotland Yard. The woman again declined to have anyone sent for. In a few minutes the sergeant returned and proceeded to take formal depositions from the two witnesses of the murder.

"My name is Colton," the woman said. "My husband's name was George Colton; he is a jeweller off Bond-street."

The sergeant looked quickly at her. He recognised the name as that of one of the oldest and most reputable firms in London.

"We live at 82 Cadogan-square, Kensington. Tonight we dined with Mrs. Martha Royce in Windsor. She is an old friend of my husband's and wanted him to take some jewels of hers to town for appraisal and I believe for sale. I begged him not to take them, to have a guard sent for them, but he laughed at me. He had often carried large amounts in jewels. Now they're gone, and he's gone."

She shivered and drew her ermine wrap closer about her slender shoulders. The sergeant's pen scratched slowly along the paper. He turned to the chauffeur.

"Your name."

"Oliver Peskett. Driver for Mr. George Colton, 82 Cadogan-square, Kensington."

"Age?"

"Thirty-one."

"How long in present employ?"

"Two years Michaelmas."

The sergeant grunted as he noted these facts down.

"Now tell me again exactly what happened," he went on. After Mrs. Colton and the chauffeur had slowly repeated the story of the robbery and murder, and the sergeant had carefully blotted his record, he said, "There's one thing more I'd like to ask you. Your husband carried jewels belonging to Mrs. Royce of Windsor, and they were stolen. Can you tell me the value, or the approximate value, of the jewels? And what were they like?"

"I can't describe them."

"You hadn't seen them?"

"No."

"But you're sure he had them? They were talked about at dinner?"

"Yes. They talked about them then and I know he had them in the black satchel. I think they were all diamonds, and I think they said the value was something like twenty or thirty thousand pounds."

The sergeant looked at the chauffeur. "You knew about them?" he said in a matter-of-fact voice.

"Not I," the chauffeur said promptly. "Hadn't the foggiest. I knew he had the bag. I didn't know what he had in it."

"All right."

The sergeant hesitated a moment. Then he said, "I won't keep you any longer. We'll take care of your husband's remains, Mrs. Colton. Will you be in your home in the morning, please. We'll want to see you again. You're sure you don't want me to send for some relative, or friend?"

She shook her head.

"No, thanks. I have no one."

The chauffeur held the door open for her. As he closed it his eyes met the steady gaze of the sergeant for an instant and quickly shifted away.

CHAPTER TWO

Inspector Bull entered the front door of his modern semi-detached villa in Hampstead. The odour of burned mutton met him full in the face, and he wished for the hundredth time that Mrs. Bull would come back home. In the two years of his married life he had failed to learn why it was that when his wife was at home the maid was what is commonly called a treasure, and when his wife was away she became an increasing liability with every meal. He took off his heavy brown overcoat, which made him somewhat resemble a large cinnamon bear on its hind legs. Not that Inspector Bull was ungainly; he was simply of large bulk. And he always wore cinnamon brown overcoats. His wife's tactful efforts to make him go in for contrasting instead of harmonising shades met a placid but adamant resistance. The tawny hazel of his moustache and his hair set the pitch for the colour harmony that Inspector Bull followed with some determination. There was no affectation or foppishness about it. Inspector Bull simply dressed in brown.

He deposited his coat and hat in the hall cupboard and went upstairs to the back room he liked to call his den. As a matter of fact that is pretty much what it was. It was pleasantly dim there. The green-shaded lamp on the large flat top desk (from Maple's) made very little headway against the dark tan paper and heavy leather upholstered furniture and the red and green turkey rug (also from Maple's). Here Bull brought and—in a sense—buried the bones of his calling as a valued member of the C.I.D. Here also came the few odds and ends of antique china that he could not resist buying from time to time. His passion for broken china had always made him the butt of the perpetual bromide about bulls in china shops. No one had ever failed to mention it. At one time Bull had smiled painfully, but that was when he was a younger man. He was now thirty-six.

He knocked out his pipe into the patented non-tipoverable ash receiver that somebody had given him and sat down in the big chair in front of his desk. He was very low. His wife was away and Scotland Yard was as dead as a door nail. Three communists and two cat burglars had constituted his entire share for two weeks. He was tired of routine, and he was especially tired of hearing about a first-rate poisoning case that Inspector Millikan had been given.

After some thought Inspector Bull reached for the telephone and called his friend, former landlord and ardent admirer Mr. Evan Pinkerton, to invite him to stay a week.

Mr. Pinkerton lived in a large dingy house in Golders Green. He was a grey mouse-like little Welshman who on one memorable occasion had emerged from his chrysalis and for a few moments had become the gaily colored butterfly, so to speak, of avenging justice. Inspector Bull had never forgot that except for the little man in Golders Green the girl who later became his wife would have been lying dead in a ravine in the mountains of Wales. In the past few years Bull had come to rely on Mr. Pinkerton's curious, almost feminine—or so Bull thought—intuition, in hard cases. He was constantly taking all the policeman's elaborately collected evidence, looking at it and saying, "Well, well, maybe it's as you say. But I should have thought the fellow with the brown toupee did it." This Inspector Bull would never admit. But he would set to work again, and with indomitable thoroughness build up another chain of evidence that led inevitably to the conviction of the man with the brown toupee. On such occasions Mr. Pinkerton would nod his head without complacency and say, "That's what I would have thought."

When Inspector Bull called up on this occasion Mr. Pinkerton allowed himself to hope that he was being invited to take part in another case. The cinema and Inspector Bull's cases were the two scarlet mountain peaks on the dull grey monotonous prairie of Mr. Pinkerton's existence. Nevertheless he carefully finished his tea of bloater and apple and plum jam before he took off his felt slippers and put on his boots. Then he washed up his dishes and left the place spotless for the woman who came in to clean for him in the mornings.

He got out the bright new suitcase the Bulls had given him for Christmas and packed his things for his visit. Next he locked all the windows, put on his brown bowler hat and his grey overcoat and took his way to Hampstead, where he found Inspector Bull sprinkling weed-killer on the lawn. People who were accustomed to read Dr. Freud would have seen an unconscious connection between the weed-killer and Inspector Millikan's poisoning case, but Inspector Bull had never read Dr. Freud, nor had Mr. Pinkerton. They greeted each other solemnly and Inspector Bull said that dinner was ready.

The downstairs clock had just struck ten, and Inspector Bull had just yawned and thought of another day of routine on the Embankment, when the telephone on his desk jangled urgently. He looked at it expectantly. It was a private connection with New Scotland Yard.

"Bull speaking!" ("Bellowing, he means," Commissioner Debenham had once remarked.) "Colnbrook? Bucks. Robbery? Murder? Right you are."

He put the receiver down and turned to his guest, whose eyes were protruding with pleasurable anticipation.

"There's been robbery and murder out on the Colnbrook Road. Chief wants me to have a look at it. He says in the morning, but I think I'll have a look at it now. You want to come along?"

No need to ask. The little man had his brown bowler and grey overcoat on before Bull had heaved his vast bulk out of his desk chair.

"I'll bring the car around," said the Inspector. "You lock the door."

In Commissioner Debenham's room at New Scotland Yard Chief Inspector Dryden and the Commissioner himself were having what in two less moderate men might be called a decided difference of opinion.

"Our method is wrong, sir," the Chief Inspector said flatly. "We've got to use modern methods for modern crime. The old tradition of the Yard is all right, but when you've got motor bandits you've got to use their own methods to get them."

The Commissioner pursed his lips and nodded his qualified agreement.

"That's undoubtedly true, to a certain extent," he replied deliberately, pushing a box of cigars across the desk. "But what can we do? Look at this business tonight. I dropped in here half an hour ago. There was a call from Colnbrook. A man with a motorcycle held up George Colton's car—the jeweller. Relieved him of a satchel of jewels, shot him dead and disappeared. Twenty minutes later we get word of it. All the motor cars in England, each one full of police, won't help us to catch that man on that motorcycle in London tonight. As soon as we hear about it we have everyone on the lookout. This is early closing day; one-third of the shopkeepers' assistants in Middlesex are out motorcyling.—Of course, if we'd known in five minutes, we could have done something. Now, new methods won't help us. It's a case of the right man on the job."

The Chief Inspector stared at the smoke rising from the end of his cigar.

"Then why, sir," he said with a polite impatience, "put Humphrey Bull on the case? Nobody likes Bull better than I do, or thinks more of his ability in certain lines; but it doesn't run to gang crime."

"Is this gang crime, Dryden?"

"Typically American, sir. The exact way it's done. The cold brutality of the gangster. Sheer, deliberate murder."

Commissioner Debenham shook his head.

"You have American crime and American methods on the brain. We'll give Bull a chance at it. If it appears to be a gang of Americans, or an Americanised gang of Englishmen, you can take it yourself. I'm a little prejudiced in Bull's favour, I must admit, since he discovered that Tito Mellema murdered that woman—what's her name? La Mar. If I'm not mistaken, Inspector, you thought her death was a gang racket because she was connected with an American musical comedy."

Inspector Dryden grinned in spite of himself.

"Perhaps you're right, sir. Well, I'll be getting home. I'm sorry old Colton's dead."

12

"So am I," said the Commissioner. "There wasn't much he didn't know about precious stones, and who owns 'em, and how much they paid."

"Or when they sold them and for how much, sir."

"I'm afraid that's right too, Dryden. I hope you're not thinking, by the way, of the recent loss of Lady Blanche's emerald collar, which rightfully belongs—or belonged—to her mother-in-law the Duchess?"

Inspector Dryden allowed himself only half a smile.

"Oh, no, sir," he said soberly.

"Of course not, Dryden. Well, we certainly got 'down the banks,' as young Boyd says, for that collar. And worse luck, I have to look in on the Home Secretary tonight, and he'll have enough to say about this business of Colton. Good-night, Inspector."

CHAPTER THREE

It was a little after eleven that night when Inspector Bull and Mr. Pinkerton drove up to the Colnbrook police station in Inspector Bull's open Morris Oxford. It had begun to rain in torrents, but Bull had refused to take the time to put up the curtains. Cold and wet, he and Mr. Pinkerton listened with impassive silence to the sergeant's account of the holdup and murder. At least Inspector Bull did, in the best manner of the Metropolitan police. Mr. Pinkerton's attempt to appear impassive was a little comical; he was quivering like a badly bred hound at the kill. The sergeant in the meantime had learned for the first time from Inspector Bull the importance of the victim that Fate had left on his doorstep, and was little short of interested himself.

"Well, we'd better run down and have a look," Bull said when the man had finished. "This rain'll leave everything a blank. What time did you phone in to have the London Road watched?"

"About 9.35, sir."

The sergeant tended to be a little aggressive, without particularly being able to think of anything he had left undone. But he had told his story ten times in the last hour, and Inspector Bull was the only person not impressed.

"Any report come in?"

"No, sir."

"Did you notify the station at Slough?"

The sergeant looked bewildered.

13

"He was headed for London!" he replied with some vexation.

Bull grunted. "If I was him," he said calmly, "I'd have turned left into the by-pass and gone right through Slough, or anywheres else, and left the people at Cranford still waiting. But I guess he could have got to Dover by the time we heard about it. Let's get along."

A lone constable in a rubber cape was on guard in the road.

"That's the place," the sergeant said.

Bull turned his overcoat collar up around his neck and got heavily out of the small car. It was pitch dark except for the small sea of light from their headlights. The sergeant explained.

"The man stopped by the gate there and waited until they came along. When the car came, he stepped out and held up his hand. The driver stopped and asked what he wanted. He found himself looking in a gun. He gets out and holds up his hands. The man orders Colton to get out. The lady is to stay where she was—she'd started to get out too, you see?"

Bull grunted.

"The car was right here?"

"That's right. The man stood here, and the driver stood just here. Then the woman takes a revolver out of the pocket in the car and fires at him. The fellow shoots twice straight into Colton. He drops right forward here. Then he's off on the cycle."

Bull grunted at this second recital and made a rapid examination, with the help of his pocket lamp, of the entrance in which the man had stood while waiting. The rain washing down the brick walk made a small sea at the side of the road. So far as Bull could make out, there was no evidence that either a man or a machine had ever stood there.

"There's one point, Inspector," the sergeant went on judicially. "That's how did he know the car with those diamonds was coming this way? It's the first thing on wheels that's not a touring lay-out that we've seen here for a month of Sundays. You know the by-pass takes 'em all around the other way."

Inspector Bull's grunt was even less interested than usual.

"Has anybody been by here while you've been on duty?" he asked the constable.

"No, sir. Only the 102 bus from Windsor. No private cars."

"And nobody on a motor-bike, I suppose."

"No, sir."

14

Bull chewed his lower lip.

"Colton was standing right here when he was shot?"

"That's the spot, sir," said the sergeant. He pointed to what Mr. Pinkerton could imagine was still the tinge of crimson that nature, in her inexorable cleanliness, had washed away with swift torrents of rain.

"Where is the body now?" Bull asked.

"Had it taken to Slough, sir. We don't have much room in the village for that sort of thing." The sergeant's voice suggested a certain fastidiousness. People seldom died in Colnbrook; no one was murdered.

"Right. We'll push along then. You might keep your man here till morning. Somebody might show up. Ready, Pinkerton?"

The little man was standing in the gateway where the killer had stood. He was dripping wet, but his eyes were bright. He decided that what he wanted to say could wait.

At Slough Inspector Bull lifted the sheet from the dead face of George Colton, jeweller by appointment to half the royal heads, crowned and decrowned, of Europe. He knew something of the history of the man on the cold marble slab in front of him. If he hadn't, he thought then, he could almost have guessed it from the prosperous well-fed look, some of which lingered even in death. The round smooth discreet face had settled into the complacent mask of the successful London merchant. For that was what George Colton had been, exclusive of everything else.

Five generations of Coltons had done business over the same counter of the little shop off Bond-street. They had done better business in the little upper room across a table made from one of Mr. Chippendale's designs done especially for Mr. George Colton, jeweller to his Majesty, in 1750. The alliances and mésalliances of half the great houses of Europe had been sealed for two hundred years by a priceless bauble from the little shop. It hardly ever changed. The Coltons ceased to reside in the little rooms above the shop sometime in the Eighties; and in 1910 they were virtually forced, by their assurance agent, to put up steel shutters. Otherwise things were much the same over a hundred years. The Colton business was small in number of transactions, but large when they counted the year's profits. If a customer paid before a year had passed—so people said—they added twenty-five per cent. for the embarrassment of lowering the standard of their clientele; otherwise they added ten per cent. for credit.

Inspector Bull did not know all this. He only knew that Colton was reputed to be one of the most prosperous jewellers of London, his firm highly solvent and above all immaculately respectable; that he was dead—murdered, in fact; that he had been robbed of a collection of diamonds reputed to have considerable value; and that it was Inspector Bull's job first to find the murderer and second to recover the jewels. He knew the habits of jewel thieves well enough to know that the two things weren't necessarily synonymous. Quite probably the continental police would put their hands on the jewels if they turned up abroad; or it was conceivable that one of the London fences might handle them. But Inspector Bull knew very well that the Commissioner would be concerned with the man who had done the thing rather than the jewels. Scotland Yard still regards human life as of more importance than precious stones. If such an outrage went unpunished, the highways of England would be as dangerous as the tracks of the jungle.

Bull looked at the collection of small articles taken from the dead man's pockets. A watch, a card case, a few notes, a handful of silver, a key ring with ordinary house keys, a handkerchief. The only article of interest the local sergeant kept, with the instinct of a showman, until the last.

"He wore this around his neck, sir."

It was a single small gold key attached to a long flat black cord.

"I'll take that," said Bull quickly. He examined it, then put it in his pocket. "In fact, I'll take the other keys too. By Jove!" he added, and then reached for the telephone.

"Bull speaking," he said when he had got Scotland Yard. "Have you got a man detailed at the Colton shop in St. Giles-street?"

He listened intently for a minute. Then he hung up the receiver.

"Well, I'm damned," said Inspector Bull mildly.

Mr. Pinkerton looked at him with bright expectant eyes.

"A man was detailed at the shop at half-past ten," Bull said placidly. "But P. C. Maxim is on point duty there. He reports that at five minutes to ten a man entered the shop by the front door, with a key. Maxim was going past when the man opened the door. The man said 'Good evening,' and asked Maxim to stand by for a minute till he came out, so he wouldn't have to lock up behind him. He was inside three minutes or so, came out, said good-bye to P. C. Maxim, and walked off."

"That's *very* interesting," Mr. Pinkerton said eagerly.

16

CHAPTER FOUR

Inspector Bull was in his small room on the Embankment before eight o'clock the next morning.

The papers he had gathered in on his way from Hampstead were unpleasantly full of sensational news.

"Lone Bandit Robs and Murders Jeweller."

"Scotland Yard Powerless to Cope with New Conditions, says Expert."

Bull put them aside wearily. He especially disliked the constant comparison of London and certain well-known American cities. To accuse Scotland Yard of inefficiency was one thing—after all it wasn't necessarily inefficient not to have caught a murderer or a bandit within twelve hours of the act. It was quite another thing to liken London to Chicago. Englishmen should have more pride.

He had to admit, however, that reports were not encouraging. Nineteen motor bicyclists had been picked up during the night. One in Maidstone was a hairdresser, coming back from seeing his young woman in Pimlico. One in Staines was a draper returning from he preferred not to tell where near Kingston. Near Oxford an undergraduate out without permission had been first detained and then turned over to the proctors. In Hounslow William Archer, occupation and age uncertain, had been playing darts to such an extent that he had forgot his way home. But no one who, as far as could be seen, had been within three miles of Colnbrook since Midsummer.

"They'll be cabling to say they've got him in Canada before noon," Inspector Bull groaned, pushing the reports aside and wondering how soon he could decently call on Mrs. Colton.

When Chief Inspector Dryden objected to the Commissioner's putting Bull in charge of what the papers came to call "the Colnbrook Outrage," he was objecting on purely professional grounds. Inspector Bull's position at the Yard was, in a sense, unique. Like all professional policemen and unlike all amateur detectives of fiction, Bull was sober, matter-of-fact, infinitely painstaking, and as shy as a colt of anything that smacked of the brilliant or the miraculous. He did not believe in mysteries. To Humphrey Bull the world was about as plain as a pikestaff. When the brilliant amateur of Jermyn-street showed, by the closest marshalling of the facts and the

17

most logical deduction from them, that Queenie La Mar could not have been poisoned by arsenic because she had not taken any, Inspector Bull, being reliably informed that her symptoms were precisely those of arsenical poisoning, very ploddingly had her exhumed and analysed, and found arsenic in her hair, nails and internal organs. He then proceeded to go over her diet again. In thus examining into what she ate, he corroborated the discovery of the brilliant amateur that like most modern young women she ate practically nothing. Still, the facts were the facts; and Inspector Bull recalled what he had learned by observation of Mrs. Bull, that even if modern young women avoid all other forms of fat, they steadily eat small but adequate quantities of lip stick. And Queenie La Mar (whose real name is not important) used more lip stick than any woman in London. Bull confiscated the cosmetics from Queenie La Mar's sealed rooms, and soon after a man ended his life in the small house in Pentonville. As Bull explained to his wife, "You see, if it isn't one thing it must be something else." It was all plain.

As a matter of fact Bull, for all his simple and matter-of-fact attitude towards his occupation, was at heart both credulous and romantic. His wife, in the fashion of wives, was unable to see how he ever managed as well as he did. Anyone could sell him anything, for instance. A manly fear of his wife's amusement was all that kept him safe from every dealer in old china in town. And he had deeply ingrained in him the prejudices of his class and of his profession. For example, one of the maxims he had learned when he first became a member of the Metropolitan police was "Be careful of women in a house of trouble." Yet with all his experience of that truth, he was never convinced that a woman, in any of his own cases, had played any rôle but that of mouse to someone else's cat. When Mr. Pinkerton had forced him to admit, in one of his most celebrated and puzzling cases, that the vicar's widow had poisoned the choir master, he convicted her. No one was more relieved when that sweet-faced old lady died a natural death before she was hanged; and in his heart of hearts Bull was convinced that it was the choir master's own fault.

In his way Inspector Bull was a specialist. He knew the impulses and motives of the great middle class, from which occasionally a great criminal springs, more unerringly than any other man at the Yard. As they used to say at the Yard, Bull was useless in St. James's or St. Giles, Mayfair or Whitechapel. But in his own field no one reached so infallibly into the inner motives of those who had broken the law of God or man. Queenie La Mar was Drury-lane—but her father was a draper in Earl's-court; and Tito Mellema's father (Titus Mellinovski) had brought up Tito, very inadequately, in the area of his interior decorating and wall paper establishment in Camden-town. Inspector Bull knew, though he could never have said it, that a middle class soul is a middle class soul, and when it commits murder in Drury-lane, Elephant and Castle or Half Moon-street, it does it from middle class motives and usually with middle class weapons.

That was why Chief Inspector Dryden did not want Bull to have the Colnbrook Outrage. It was clearly outside his field. But the Commissioner had decided it; and at ten o'clock, when Bull called on Mrs. George Colton, he was well launched into dangerous seas.

Mrs. Colton was in her sitting room when Bull was announced. He looked hesitatingly at the slim graceful young woman with clear hazel eyes and smoothly waved ash-blonde hair standing by the fire-place.

"Is Mrs. Colton . . . ?"

"I am Mrs. Colton." Her voice was slightly husky and vaguely disturbing. "Will you sit down?"

Inspector Bull was slightly embarrassed. He realized how many preconceived notions he had brought with him. Quite unconsciously he had made up a picture of George Colton's home life, built around the image of the plump, pink, well-nourished jowls of the dead jeweller. The discreet complacency, the shrewd respectability of that dead face were in the oddest contrast with the pale lovely woman in black sitting across from him, regarding him thoughtfully out of calm sad eyes. She could not be more than twenty-seven or eight, Bull thought. As he sat down he forgot, with admirable adaptability, the fat, weeping, bejewelled old lady he had expected to meet.

He got out his notebook.

"I've heard the principal facts about this, Mrs. Colton," he said a little awkwardly. "I would like to know first, now, how many people knew your husband had the jewels with him last night."

Mrs. Colton showed no surprise. She thought for a moment.

"*I* knew it," she said then. "I don't know surely how many others did. Mrs. Royce, of course. And her son too. That's all I'm sure of."

19

"Your chauffeur?"

"I think he didn't know. Surely if he had he wouldn't have stopped the car."

"Do you think it's out of the question, madam, that he knew the man in the road?"

She looked at him quickly.

"Oh, that's absurd. He's been with us over two years. My husband trusted him in everything."

"What about the other servants?"

"That's out of the question too. My husband never discussed his affairs with anyone. I knew quite by accident that he had the jewels with him. I came into the drawing room at Mrs. Royce's when she was taking his receipt for them. I tried to persuade him to send a guard out for them today. Mrs. Royce thought I was silly and so did Mr. Colton."

"Yes. Who is Mrs. Royce, please?"

Inspector Bull was writing industriously in his notebook, but he was thinking about something else.

"She is an old friend of my husband's. I think her husband and Mr. Colton went to school together. He died many years ago and left her well-to-do. Then someone else died about ten years ago and left her more money. My husband of course thought diamonds were a sound investment and persuaded her to buy. The gold-in-the-stocking theory of economics, I suppose you call it."

Inspector Bull looked up at her.

"Yes. I understand from your statement last night that she was thinking of selling. Had she decided that diamonds were not such a good investment, or did she need money?"

Mrs. Colton smiled faintly. "I don't know, Mr.—Inspector —Bull. She doesn't need money, however, and of course diamonds have gone down considerably. Perhaps she thought she'd better unload before they went down more. In fact I remember now my husband did say he'd advised her to sell."

"When was that, madam?"

"On the way to Colnbrook. After we'd left Windsor. They have gone down four shillings in the pound, I think he said. Something of the sort."

"Yes. Do you know if they had agreed on last night, previously, as the time he was to get them?"

"I suppose they had. They were to be appraised in Hatton-garden this morning."

"Who by?" asked Bull quickly.

She thought a moment.

"Would it be Mr. Steiner?" she asked. "I barely heard the name mentioned. It seems like a good name."

A half-smile appeared for a fleeting second on her lips. Inspector Bull looked at her placidly. The occasion of her amusement passed him by. He noted down two words: "Albert Steiner."

"Then Mr. Colton was arranging a sale?" he went on.

"I think so. I suppose he probably had a purchaser. Say an American."

"Oh," said Bull.

"I don't know that," she went on a little hastily. "But my husband was a careful business man. While he was very fond of Mrs. Royce, I don't think he would have undertaken to sell some old-fashioned stones for her unless he could do it easily. If it was just an idea they'd have done it long ago—I should think. That's why I think he had a buyer in mind. And I suppose it was an American because everyone else is poor. It's just guess-work."

Inspector Bull wrote in the black notebook.

"If it is true, Mrs. Colton," he said, "there are a good many people who could have known he had the jewels that night."

She hesitated, and looked reflectively out of the window.

"Yes . . . and no, Inspector. Mr. Steiner, if that's his name, knew they were to be brought to him this morning, I suppose. I don't know that he knew my husband was bringing them personally from Windsor last night. Or even that he knew they were in Windsor."

"What about your husband's clerks, madam?"

Again the half-smile, quickly vanishing.

"My husband's clerk is Mr. Smith," she said very seriously. "He would probably know about it. He's seventy-four and he's been with the firm longer than my husband had. Then there's the boy. His name is Gates. He wouldn't know."

Inspector Bull only looked his question.

"Because he only polishes the silver and opens the door. You see, he's just fifty."

In spite of himself Bull glanced up at her. In his earnest fashion he had thought he detected an unbecoming levity in her voice. But she was perfectly composed. There was even a trace of distinct unhappiness in the calm eyes.

Then as she caught his glance she said impulsively, "Oh, you see it's always seemed so absurd to me—all the fuss and bother about shop and important clients and all of it. I only persuaded my husband to stop wearing a top hat and dress like a human being a few months ago. Oh, it's ghastly, all of it."

The mask of composure had slipped a little, and Inspector

Bull was glad of it. The eyes flashed, and again there was a glint of pain in them.

"I see," he said soberly. "How many people are there in Mrs. Royce's household?"

"There's her son. He, by the way, brought the jewels from the vault in the Midland Bank in Windsor yesterday afternoon."

"Then he knew her plans about them?"

"I don't know, I'm sure."

"If he did, that makes five people who knew about them, including yourself. Steiner of Hatton-garden; Mrs. Royce; her son; your husband's clerk Smith. Your driver makes a possible sixth, and I suppose there are servants in the Royce house who could have overheard something. Then there's a chance that somebody at the bank talked about it."

The telephone at the low table beside Mrs. Colton's chair rang.

"Hello. Oh, yes, Mr. Field. Yes, if you will. I didn't want to disturb you last night. Very well. Thank you."

She turned to Bull.

"It's my husband's solicitor. He's coming out now. He can tell you about my husband's affairs. I suppose he might even know who was going to buy the stones."

"I'll have to see him later, madam," Inspector Bull said, getting to his feet. "Just one more point. Please give me the best description you can of the man who stopped you in the Colnbrook Road."

She shrugged her shoulders helplessly.

"I've tried so hard to remember what he was like! But I can't, except vaguely. He was about my husband's height and not so heavy; and that's really all I can think of about him. If I'd only not tried to help! When we started out my husband took the revolver out of his pocket and said, 'You see how silly it is to be alarmed. I'll put this here in sight.' He put it in the pocket by the arm rest. When he didn't take it I reached for it. I thought I could frighten the man. Then I nearly fainted. That's really all I know."

Bull put his notebook in his pocket.

"Thank you. I'll trouble you as little as I can. I'd like to see the chauffeur now, please."

She rang the bell. "Do you want him to come here?"

"I'll see him in the garage, please."

Mrs. Colton directed the maid to take Inspector Bull to see the chauffeur. Inspector Bull followed the trim little maid mechanically, thinking of several things very hard. They went out a side door towards the back of the house. Bull

22

suddenly noticed that the maid was surreptitiously looking at him, as they went along, with intense curiosity, shaking with excitement. They came around a corner of the house.

"Ah!" the maid whispered suddenly. "There's Peskett now, talking to Miss Agatha."

Bull saw a man of middle size standing by a large Daimler in the driveway. He was looking sullenly at the ground and kicking pebbles along the drive. A young woman was talking urgently to him.

As Bull advanced the girl turned quickly around and came forward. She was about twenty-five, Bull thought, rather pretty, with black eyes, dark curling hair and a mouth closed as tightly as a steel trap. Without looking at Bull she went quickly into the house by an open french window.

"Who's that?" Bull said to the maid, who was standing by the corner of the house.

"Oh, sir, that's Miss Agatha. The master's daughter, sir."

Bull went along to the driveway where Peskett was polishing the windows of the big car. He could not see the two pairs of eyes that were watching him through lace curtains. One pair of calm hazel eyes upstairs, one pair of burning black eyes behind the french window.

"I'd like to talk to you a minute, Peskett," he said. "I'm Inspector Bull of Scotland Yard."

CHAPTER FIVE

Peskett was not the type of man that Bull would have picked for George Colton's chauffeur. He was clearly not the sort of man to touch his cap and hold the door open with any kind of grace or suavity, even for a very respectable and prosperous merchant. Servants generally, male servants in particular, belong to that great class of people whose public and private lives have no connection with each other . . . like labour cabinet ministers, and interior decorators whose fathers are dukes. Publicly and privately their set-ups are as different as Fulham-road and Grosvenor-square. When they disappear from the eye of their public they reach a different plane of feeling and conduct; when they reappear they wear a mask that disguises them. Oliver Peskett was not like that, Inspector Bull thought. He could not place him.

"I want you to tell me about last night, Peskett."

He conceded, in spite of whatever ideas he might have

23

had from a first sight of the man, that the chauffeur's story was simple, direct and explicit. Though not in exactly the same words, it differed in no essential, as far as Bull could remember, from the statement taken at the police station in Colnbrook and from that just given him by Mrs. Colton.

When Peskett had finished Bull thought it over a moment.

"What did you do when he shot?" he asked.

"I didn't do anything," Peskett said. "I didn't want to get shot myself, and I didn't have a gun. I don't think he would have fired if Mrs. Colton had kept her head. He didn't look as if he meant to, anyway. I suppose she thought she'd scare him off."

Bull thought again.

"How much were those diamonds worth?"

"I heard Mrs. Colton tell the sergeant at Colnbrook they were worth around £30,000."

"That's the first you knew of it?"

"That's right."

"But you knew he was carrying jewels of some value?"

"I didn't. Nothing of the sort. I knew when I saw him get in the car at Windsor that he had jewels with him. He always carried them in that little black satchel. The day he took the Austrian crown jewels to Cheltenham to show them to Lady Morgan that's the way he carried them. But I carried a gun that day. Some of those roads are pretty lonesome. He thought it was foolish. I never could figure him out about that."

"Did he carry stones about often, in that satchel?"

"Never saw him carry them any other way, and I've been driving him two years."

Bull wondered if he noticed a shade of defiance in the man's voice.

"You weren't armed last night, though?" he asked.

"Mr. Colton wouldn't have it. Sometimes I used to take a gun without his knowing it, when I knew he had stones with him. I didn't know he would, last night, so I didn't have one. I guess it wouldn't have been much good anyway. That fellow was pretty quick on the draw."

Bull looked at him with a hardly perceptible but increased interest.

"Where are you from, by the way?"

"I came to Mr. Colton from Manchester."

"Born there?"

"No. I worked there from 1919 on."

"What doing?"

"I drove a lorry for Weber and Ernst."

24

"You say Mr. Colton was opposed to firearms. Do you mean he didn't carry them himself, or didn't want you to?"

"Both. He said they invited murder. I guess he thought more about his hide than he did of money. That's saying a lot."

"How do you account for the gun he had in the side pocket of the car last night?"

Perhaps the placidity of Inspector Bull's tone had the slightest dangerously silky quality.

The driver gave a short mirthless laugh.

"I don't. I could swear he never had one there before."

"When the man stopped you, you didn't see he was masked until you let down the window, I understand."

"That's right. Then I saw he had a couple of guns. I did just what I was told."

"You must have had time to get a pretty fair idea of what he was like, didn't you?"

"Yes and no."

Peskett hesitated a little.

"I couldn't see his face at all, you see. Cap over his forehead, goggles over his eyes, mask over the rest. But I thought of one thing. His voice was faked, it was too deep. He was putting on, if you know what I mean. And he bit off his words, like he didn't want to talk any more than he had to."

Inspector Bull thought hard about that.

"What else?" he said.

"Well, he was taller than Mr. Colton. Then there was something about him. I don't know what it was. But I'd know him if I saw him again."

Bull looked at him thoughtfully. "What kind of a machine did he have?"

"Dunlop four."

"Did you see it?"

"No. Heard it."

"You know a lot about motorcycles?"

"I know enough to know what kind of an engine it's got when I hear it go."

"What did Miss Colton want out here a minute ago?"

The driver reached in his pocket for a cigarette. There was a noticeable hesitation.

"She wanted to know why I happened to take the Colnbrook Road instead of the by-pass," he said then.

The faint glint of amusement in Inspector Bull's eyes did strange things to his stolid, simple face.

"That's just what I was going to ask you myself," he said pleasantly.

"And I was going to tell you just what I told her," the driver said calmly. "That Mr. Colton told me to take it when we left Windsor. I suppose he wanted to keep away from that place on the by-pass where there's been three hold-ups the last fortnight."

Bull nodded. "Reason enough, too. Well, good-morning. I'll be seeing you later."

He got into his car and set off for Windsor, with the germs of several ideas tucked away safely in his mind.

"Mr. Peskett isn't as clever as he thinks," Inspector Bull thought with some complacency.

CHAPTER SIX

Mrs. Royce lived, so Inspector Bull discovered without much trouble, in a four-storey red brick Georgian house in the Windsor High-street. She would have preferred to live in one of her houses in the country—she had two, with adequate funds for maintenance and operation—but her principles would not permit it. Mrs. Royce believed that it was someone's duty to protect the rear view of the royal household. When new tea-shops were opened in the High-street she wrote letters to the *Times*. Her letters seemed not to deter Messrs. Lyons, or whoever it might be, but they exhibited Mrs. Royce doing her duty as a British subject. She refused all offers for her own house with great violence. Once, Bull learned, she had called in a surprised constable to eject a still more surprised London agent who had not fully realised that she really did not mean to sell.

Mrs. Royce—though Inspector Bull would not have put it this way—was an Edwardian. Edwardians are much worse than Victorians, for the reason that when they reverted to type after the wicked but thin veneering of the gay Nineties they reverted even further than type. More than that, they had had a sip of life, and knew just how heady a drink it really was. This the Victorians in their innocence had only guessed.

Mrs. Royce had had a gay youth. A royal prince had passed her house every morning for a week just to catch a glimpse of her. That was in 1887. She had managed to push a kitten out of the drawing-room window. The Prince had actually picked it up and returned it to her. Mrs. Royce thus knew very well how dangerous life could be, and how delightful. So when, in her middle age, she started to go native

26

—for surely the Victorians are the quintessence of Englishness—she went native with a vengeance. She became a veritable dragon. Only a sharp observer could see a fiery twinkle in the old grey eyes under the grizzled Lily Langtry coiffure.

Mrs. Royce wore heavy purple grosgrain silk dresses with beaded collars in the winter, and lavender grosgrain silk dresses with a black velvet band around her neck in the summer. In the winter her hats were black velvet, resembling a section of stovepipe, topped with mink tails. In the summer they were straw with pansies. In all seasons she was a formidable figure. She never hesitated to express herself in a manner as terrifying as her person. She had once said to George Colton, her friend and business adviser, " 'Pon my soul, George, I do believe you're the only person I know in England who doesn't shiver when I appear. It's most extraordinary, 'pon my soul it is. And my own son at that."

That was true, in spite of the *non sequitur*, which was characteristic. Mr. Colton was not afraid of her; her own son was very much so, or so people thought.

"Mother's so beastly unpredictable," was his chief comment in the thirty years of his existence by her. He hardly knew, when he opened his mother's morning's mail, whether he would have a letter from her solicitor cutting him off without a shilling, or one directing him to step around to the Piccadilly show rooms to view the Mercedes she had ordered for him.

When Inspector Bull arrived mother and son were, it appeared, in the upstairs drawing room. He was shown up. It was a room after his own heart. Everything on which an *objet* could be placed was covered, and draped landscapes and portraits on easels, sofas and chairs with velvet fringes and white antimacassars, palms, aspidistras, huge Chinese vases, and elaborate screens with portraits in the panels completely filled the room except for a narrow passage that led from each door to a small clear space, like an oasis (with palms outside) in the centre. Into this space Inspector Bull tried to insinuate his great bulk without tipping anything, or everything, over.

Mrs. Royce sat in state against her formidable background. Bull could not see her very clearly, he discovered. The heavy, long, dark green silk window drapes were partly drawn, giving to a naturally light room a depressing twilight gloom. That in spite of the fact that outside the sun was shining mildly—indeed brightly, for February.

Her son was standing behind her. It was obvious that he felt no more at home in his mother's drawing room than Bull did. He was a discordant note, Bull felt at once; even more so than the expensive wireless set in the corner behind a section of the palms.

"So you're the police, young man!"

Bull almost jumped at the sound of that deep bass voice. He had never felt so keenly his personal inadequacy to represent New Scotland Yard.

"And have you found my diamonds? And who killed George Colton, eh?"

"Not yet, ma'am," Bull said.

"Well, my son says you never will. Not that I take much stock in what *he* says."

She stared belligerently at him.

"We'll do our best, ma'am," he said, recovering what was his best approximation to some sort of professional suavity. "And I'd like any information you can give me."

"Information indeed," said Mrs. Royce. "That's your business, my good man, not mine."

Bull found himself actively disliking Mrs. Royce. He always and above all things hated to be called "my good man." It made him unaccountably angry.

"It will save me time, ma'am," he said stolidly, "if you will answer a few questions."

Mrs. Royce breathed heavily. Inspector Bull got out his black notebook. Mrs. Royce shook her grizzled curls almost savagely. "Very well!" she said.

"What was the value of the jewels Mr. Colton had last night, please?"

"The assurance people can tell you that better than I can, I'm sure. That's *their* business. You know as well as I do that with the market what it is it's hard to say what anything's worth."

"Then approximately, ma'am," Inspector Bull said patiently.

"Between £20,000 and £30,000, I'm told."

"Were they fully insured against theft?"

"Of course they were. With the police what they are you have to insure your false hair."

Mrs. Royce nodded her old head at him with the grimmest of smiles.

Bull had no gift of repartee, which partly explained his considerable success as a policeman. When unduly goaded he managed, through no particular merit of his own—or none that he would have been aware of—to give the impression of a Newfoundland ignoring the yapping of a Mexican hairless. Not that Mrs. Royce resembled such an animal in the least. Now he managed to remain imperturbable—until,

28

glancing at young Mr. Royce, he saw a twinkle of amusement in his eye. Inspector Bull gave him a glance of placid dislike.

"Who beside yourself knew that Mr. Colton was taking the jewels to town last night, Mrs. Royce?" he said stolidly.

"Mrs. Colton, I suppose. That scatter-brained wife of his. In my time, I can tell you, sensible men didn't discuss their business with their wives."

Bull nodded, easily understanding such a reticence on the part of the deceased Mr. Royce. There was a second flicker in the younger man's eyes.

"My son here knew. He got them from the vault yesterday afternoon. I suppose Mr. Thornton, the manager, knew. Eh, Michael?"

She turned towards Michael.

"Michael, come out here where I can see you. And, Inspector, sit down!"

Michael Royce slipped out into the cleared space. Bull sat down on a tan plush chair with castors that made it a precarious seat until his weight anchored it into the rug.

"Yes, I told Thornton, Mother. He was worried about letting them go. I told him Colton was taking them into town that night."

"Well, then. I'm sure that's all. Of course that person in Hatton-gardens may have known."

"Hatton-garden, ma'am," said Inspector Bull politely. "Mr. Steiner."

Whatever Mrs. Royce might be, Bull saw, she was not dull. She gave him a fierce stare. It was followed by a subterranean chuckle.

"You're not as big a fool as I thought you were, Inspector. What difference does it make what it's called or what he's called. I don't even know that Colton told him when he was bringing the jewels. And I'm sure that's all."

"Servants, ma'am?"

"Stuff and nonsense. Murry is sixty-five and as deaf as a post. The parlour maid is too stupid to be in an institution, much less conduct a robbery."

"Are they your only servants?"

"Don't be inane, young man. Certainly not. There's the cook, the chauffeur, and the house-maid. Out of the question."

Bull thought about it. He wondered.

Mrs. Royce continued.

"The diamonds are all very well, young man." Her voice was grim, and she fixed Bull with an unflinching eye. "But what I want to see is that ruffian hanged who shot George

Colton down in cold blood. George Colton was the best friend I ever had. When I think it was a few paltry baubles of mine that were responsible for his death, I'm ashamed, Inspector. I'm ashamed!"

Bull felt himself strangely moved just then. There was something almost gentle about the old woman. The deep hoarse voice demanding justice for her friend was curiously tender. Inspector Bull happened to glance at Michael Royce. That young man was obviously ill at ease.

CHAPTER SEVEN

Inspector Bull was distinctly uncomfortable. He was tired of hearing about the inefficiency of the police. He was even more tired of hearing their supposed inefficiency condoned on the grounds that their powers were limited by such and such an Act. At the same time he was forced to admit that, with many possibilities, he saw little positive enlightenment.

A description of the jewels by the Continental Bonding and Assurance Company, Ltd., with premises in Threadneedle-street, was on his desk when he returned to the Embankment after lunch. Also the information that the stones were insured by Mrs. Royce for £35,000. Further, that the company had put two of their private detectives on the job of recovering them.

Inspector Bull snorted, thought, got his hat and coat and called on the company's manager by way of bus from Trafalgar-square. Mr. Smedley was glad to see him. Inspector Bull, he trusted, could easily understand their position in the matter.

Bull agreed without enthusiasm.

"Mrs. Royce tells me the jewels are fully covered by your company?"

"Fully indeed," said Mr. Smedley. He had, for a second, forgot the elegance of the well-bred manager. Bull looked at him inquiringly.

"Very fully, Inspector. Very fully indeed. That's the great trouble."

Inspector Bull's mild blue eyes remained on the manager.

"Last week, Inspector, I discussed this matter with one of our directors. I told him that Mrs. Royce's diamonds were insured far beyond their present value. In spite of the decreased production—which is purely artificial—the price of diamonds has gone down twenty per cent. this year. I don't know if you know all this. Now, in addition, the efforts to bolster up present prices brought a sharp reduction in the value of old stones. For example, the fashion in cutting has changed. You know, of course, how such changes are brought about. That is particularly applicable to Mrs. Royce's stones. I should say that their present value is between £10,000 and £15,000.

"I explained that to our directors. I said I thought we were laying ourselves open to just this sort of thing."

"What action did you take?" Inspector Bull asked.

The man hesitated and rubbed his thin dry hands together.

"As a matter of fact," he said, a little reluctantly, "our Board of Directors meets Monday week. It was planned to take the matter up at that time. I would then have been directed to advise Mrs. Royce of their intentions."

Bull looked his question.

"And have the stones revalued for a reduction of the covering."

Bull nodded. This was a complication.

"And, as a matter of fact," Mr. Smedley continued, "I had asked her to have the stones reappraised herself, by a competent person, and to have him report to the directors at that meeting."

"When was it that you told her?" Bull asked.

Mr. Smedley thought.

"Four days ago."

"Is it customary to change the assessed value of property you insure?"

"This is a very unusual case, Inspector. Values have shifted since the war. We've had severe drains on our resources. We paid £150,000 to Lord Rosen after that terrible fête at Lewes Manor. Then there was the Manborough affair."

Mr. Smedley winced painfully at the memory, and lowered his voice.

"In short . . . financial situation over the country . . . we have felt it best to make . . . what shall I say?—readjustments."

"One of which," Inspector Bull summed up, "was Mrs. Royce's diamonds."

Mr. Smedley nodded.

"You see, they were insured with us before her husband's death. That was in 1910. They are a fine collection of stones, but they have no extrinsic value, and their intrinsic value has decreased sharply. I mean, there's no single great stone, or historic interest, or anything of that sort. I explained all that to Mrs. Royce. I may say that she was singularly amenable."

"She didn't object?" Inspector Bull's surprise was evident.

31

"Oh, no! Oh, no! I don't mean that at all. But in view of the . . . vigour of most of her opinions and objections, she took this proposal in extraordinary good part. Oh, she said we were outrageous robbers, and she would put her property with another concern. But she says that so often that we . . . we understand each other."

"Well," said Bull patiently, "and did she have the stones appraised?"

"That's what Mr. Colton was bringing them to town for last night. We agreed on Albert Steiner in Hatton-garden."

"I see. Did you know Colton was bringing them in last night?"

"Oh, yes. We knew it."

Mr. Smedley's answer came without hesitation. Bull wondered if he saw the point of the question. Then he wondered if, with so frequent an affirmative answer to it, the question had any point. So far he had found no one who didn't know that the jewels were being brought that night from Windsor to London. But then the idea came back to him: All very well, but why the Colnbrook Road?

"I think, Mr. Smedley," he said, "it's obvious that this was an inside job, so to speak. It wasn't an accidental robbery. Somebody knew the jewels were coming. Now who else besides yourself, in this office, knew about them?"

Mr. Smedley allowed himself a tiny smile as he rubbed his hands nervously together.

"My secretary," he said. "You can depend on her honesty."

"I'll see her, please."

Bull got his coat and hat as the manager pressed a button. A be-spectacled woman came in from an outer office. Bull looked at her and said, "Never mind."

He felt that he could, as Mr. Smedley said, depend on her honesty; she was fifty and remarkably unattractive. She was not in league with Peskett, nor with Michael Royce.

"Thank you," he said. "I understand that unless the jewels are recovered, you'll pay Mrs. Royce £35,000."

Mr. Smedley's smile was wintry.

"I'm afraid we shall," he said.

It occurred to Inspector Bull as he went out that the Thames River would be an excellent place to search for the Royce diamonds.

CHAPTER EIGHT

George Colton's shop in St. Giles-street was of the type that has almost disappeared from London. Soon the South Kensington Museum will be the only place where they can be seen. There was the eighteenth century rounding front with its small panes of heavy clouded glass that had weathered, with infrequent breakage, two hundred years of London street life. The heavy steel bars behind were as discreetly unobtrusive as it was possible to make them. Outside, the insignia of successive generations of royal patrons were small and weatherbeaten—not large, shiny and vulgar, as they are sometimes displayed by new stores. The upper storey was low, the many windows narrow and leaded. Inspector Bull knew the place very well. He supposed Mrs. Colton would sell it to Woolworth's. Still, Woolworth's would probably have no use for such a location as St. Giles. Showmanship had not been important in the dealings of Colton's. Bull wondered vaguely if he mightn't buy the old front and set it up in Hampstead. He decided it would be impracticable as well as out of place, and further that Mrs. Bull would not allow it.

He looked around for the man who was keeping an eye on the place, and spotted him leaning with ostentatious ease against a pillar-box across the street. He nodded to him and the man came over.

"Anyone been here?"

"Yes, sir. This morning early the old fellow—said he was a clerk—came. I told him what had happened. He sort of went balmy, sir."

"Where'd he go?"

"Don't know, sir. I offered to get him a cab. Said he did't want one. Just shook his head and sort of staggered off. I was sort of worried, but I couldn't leave. He turned left on Bondstreet, sir."

Bull unlocked the door with one of the keys he had got from the proprietor's pocket, and stepped inside. He found a switch and turned on the lights. It might have been a hundred years since the shop had seen human activity. It had a curious air of having always existed completely apart from the slow-moving current of life on the little street outside. Bull thought how much more neatly shop-keepers died than other people. When you were called in after a shop-keeper's death everything was already nicely put away and ready for you.

He went into the small back room. A grey cat came to meet him, and rubbed luxuriously against his leg.

"Hello!" he said, and was a little shocked at his own voice.

He looked around. There was not much furniture. Several efficient-looking modern safes stood against the wall. A dingy black alpaca jacket hung from a hook in a large cupboard. A narrow stairway led from the corner behind a small work-bench. Bull went up, thinking irrelevantly how many beaux of three centuries had climbed these steps, and how different his errand was from any of theirs.

He was in the small front room with the heavy leaded casement windows; it had a faded Turkey carpet and a little mahogany table with a black velvet cushion on it. There was a chair on one side and a stool on the other. Again Bull had a picture of the earlier days of Colton's, when Colton was a master goldsmith, and his clients wore plum-coloured velvet breeches and embroidered coats. The present—or immediately past—owner was different, and so were his clients. Bull could not imagine George Colton balanced on the stool showing a tiara to His Excellency Mr. —— of the Province of ——. But doubtless he did. Then Bull decided he didn't, when he went into one of the back rooms and saw a comfortable modern office, furnished with shiny mahogany. A small safe was set into the wall in one corner. He looked around. He was trying to find something to open with a small gold key. He preferred to find it without assistance.

Bull spent half an hour in the shop and went out as wise as he had come in. Perhaps a little wiser; he knew Frank Smith's address. He also knew where the "boy"—whose name was James B. Gates—lived, but that did not seem important at the time. Later it became so, Inspector Bull found.

In his room on the Embankment Bull frowningly drained the syrupy dregs of an enormous cup of tea, brushed the crumbs of sultana cake off his burnt sienna cravat, and prepared to tell Commissioner Debenham and Chief Inspector Dryden what he had found out about the Colnbrook Outrage—or more properly, what he had not found out.

The two were in the Commissioner's room when he went in.

"Well, Bull," said the Commissioner, "what have you done?"

Commissioner Debenham liked Bull, chiefly, he supposed, because Bull was so inordinately serious. He was always amused by Bull's reports, which read like bad mystery yarns, and by his inveterate faith in ultimate romance. The Commissioner himself had a sense of humour and knew how bad people really were. Bull, having very little, had no idea, the Commissioner insisted, of even the minor sins of mankind.

"Not much of anything, sir," said Bull. "I saw Colton. He was shot twice, once near the heart and once right through it. He died instantly. The fellow on the cycle got away clean as a whistle, of course."

"Well, what have you got?"

A slight scowl appeared on Inspector Bull's otherwise impassive large face.

"There's something funny about it, sir."

Debenham glanced across at Chief Inspector Dryden.

"I don't understand Colton's wife. She's under thirty, I think. His daughter's about the same age. Pretty and fierce, she is. Then there's the chauffeur. He's an American."

Chief Inspector Dryden glanced at the Commissioner.

"Did he tell you so, Bull?"

"No, sir. I didn't have to ask him. His looks and the way he speaks."

"Go on, Bull."

"Well, I didn't question him much, but I'm looking him up to see if he's got a record. He doesn't look like a chauffeur much. Well, they both say just what they said last night, and it sounds pretty good. I mean about the actual hold-up and shooting. They sound as if they meant it. But the driver sounds as if he meant something more, too.

"I was out there in an hour after the murder, but it'd been raining. I couldn't see anything—not even car tracks. There's no record of motorcyclists between there and town. He got away clean. But there are two funny things. The first is, why didn't Colton go on the by-pass?"

Commissioner Debenham nodded.

"It's obviously a put-up job, sir. The man on the motorbike knew exactly what was happening. They didn't say that he didn't hesitate a moment about anything, but they implied it. He *knew*. It's a nice lonely spot, that—where the Derwent-Foster place is for sale."

The Commissioner nodded again.

"Then there's point Number Two, sir. The Royces. It's the old lady's diamonds were stolen. They're worth from ten to fifteen thousand pounds and they're insured for thirty-five. Depreciation, sir. I'm going to see Albert Steiner about them at half past five this afternoon. Well, they stand to gain by that robbery. Now Mrs. Colton says she thought Colton was going to sell them. Smedley—he's the manager of Continental Bonding and Assurance—says they were going to reappraise them to cut the insurance."

The Commissioner turned to the Chief Inspector.

"Gives it a little different look, Dryden?" he said.

Dryden nodded noncommittally.

"It might just be a lucky break for the Royces, sir, as the Americans say."

"Very lucky, indeed, I'd say, sir," Bull observed. "Well, then here's the list of those that knew Colton was bringing the jewels in to town. Mrs. Royce, Michael Royce, Colton, the clerk Smith, Smedley, Albert Steiner, and perhaps the clerk Gates at Colton's. They knew a day or so before, all of them. Then Mrs. Colton knew it that night only—so she says.

"Now the driver knew Colton was carrying stones when he saw the black satchel, but not before. He didn't know their value. He says Colton was never armed. Can't explain the automatic in the side pocket of the car. Had no idea there was one there. Sometimes carried a gun himself, when he knew Colton had jewels, but always without Colton's permission. And that's about all, sir. I ought to have the report on Peskett—that's the driver—pretty soon, and I have to see Steiner now. Then I'm going to find the clerk, Smith, and see that Colton household again. This isn't as clear as it looks, sir."

Debenham nodded as Inspector Bull departed.

"Well," said Chief Inspector Dryden, "he may be right, sir. But I think it's important that that driver is an American. Some of these Americans are pretty lousy."

"Dryden," said the Commissioner, "where in God's name do you get these appalling expressions?"

Dryden grinned sheepishly.

"My son's engaged to an American college girl, sir."

"Dryden, you're just the man I've been looking for. You meet the deputation from the Philadelphia traffic division this afternoon."

CHAPTER NINE

Inspector Bull left the Commissioner's office expecting to go at once to see Albert Steiner in Hatton-garden. It was not the first time a case had taken him there; he had heard strange tales of human greed and depravity from the short enigmatic Jew, peering myopically through incredibly heavy lenses, and smiling quietly, with half the wisdom of Solomon in his dark voice, across the wide oak table in that unobtrusive shop. Mr. Steiner knew a great deal that Scotland Yard would like to know. Both Scotland Yard and Mr. Steiner knew this, but neither ever referred to it. Mr. Steiner was always willing to help the police, but, as Commissioner Debenham once remarked, Steiner was born a thousand years before Scotland Yard was thought of. Still, Bull was counting on him—for what, he did not quite know.

And yet, he did. He wanted to know precisely why they were reappraising Mrs. Royce's diamonds. There seemed to be several theories about that. If Mrs. Colton was right in believing her husband had a purchaser for them, Mrs. Royce gained £20,000 by the robbery; for, granting that Mr. Smedley was right about the depreciation, Colton could not sell them for more than £15,000; and they were insured for £35,000.

If, on the other hand, Mr. Smedley was right in thinking that Mrs. Royce had no idea of selling the stones, it was a slightly different matter. If she had decided to pocket her loss and unload, she was interested in having actual cash. If she was merely having them reappraised at the request of the assurance company, it was evident she did not need money at all.

In either case she gained, naturally, some £20,000 by their loss, and by any standard was devilishly fortunate. On the second assumption, that she had not intended to sell, she would have a great deal of money when she had expected none. On the first assumption, that she had intended to sell, she would have a great deal of money more than she had expected. In one case she might conceivably have regrets for the theft—assuming what Inspector Bull, having seen Mrs. Royce, was entirely unable to do, that she had a sentimental attachment to her jewels. In the other case she could only be delighted at her unexpected windfall. Unless—here Inspector Bull stopped with inborn and trained caution—she had expected just what she got. Was it possible . . . ?

The telephone on his desk was jangling, and Bull answered it impatiently. He wanted to be on his way to Hatton-garden.

He recognised the slow, slightly husky voice of Mrs. Colton.

"Mr. Smith, my husband's clerk, is here, Inspector Bull. He's in a very bad state. If you want to talk to him you'll have to hurry, I'm afraid."

"I'll be right along," Bull said.

He put down the receiver and took up his hat and overcoat. Mr. Steiner in Hatton-garden could wait. It seemed that Mr. Smith in Cadogan-square could not.

Bull was accustomed to the air of mystery that housemaids adopt when they admit the police. As much as to say, "Between ourselves this doesn't surprise *me*. If you'd lived here as long as *I* have you'd expect *anything* to happen in *this* house." He recognised the girl as the one he'd talked to that morning, but he had no time for her.

"I could of told him a few," she observed when she went back to the kitchen where tea was being finished. "However, if he's so high and mighty . . ."

Mrs. Coggins the cook shook her head. "You leave policemen be, my lass. It's no concern of yours."

"It's not, isn't it? Well I'd like to know whose it is, then. It's all very well to talk, but I saw Miss Agatha slip down to talk to Peskett no sooner than he got out of sight this morning. And that's not all. In five minutes down went the missus herself and talks to him. No wonder he gives hisself airs."

Mrs. Coggins shook her head more determinedly.

"It don't do a girl any good to be carrying tales. No matter *where* she carries 'em. Now you wash up and I'll go see poor Mr. Smith. Mark my words he won't last long. Coggins was took that bad and he didn't last the night."

In the library Bull saw Mrs. Colton for the second time. Why Mrs. Royce should have called her scatter-brained he could not say. She obviously was not. If anything she was too reserved, too subdued. It never entered Inspector Bull's mind that she might be grieving for her husband.

Bull of course was aware that he was a very bad judge of women. Nothing affected him as pleasantly as a beautiful one. In a completely detached way, of course. He regarded them much as he regarded the Dresden china shepherdesses he used to collect before he married one. They were to be admired from a distance. If you touched them, something always managed to come off—a hand, or a foot, or some of the brittle lace of their dresses. Or even their heads. Bull was a great believer in the dust on the butterfly's wing. Which was pretty much the way he saw Mrs. Colton.

She *was* lovely. She had warm ivory skin and deep hazel eyes, crowned (he would have said) by sleek, smoothly waved ash-blonde hair drawn into a knot low on her neck. Her voice suited her very well, Bull thought several times.

"Mr. Smith is upstairs. He seems almost exhausted. I haven't called a doctor, though. I thought rest would be enough for him. Will you go up now?"

"Yes. When did he come?"

"This afternoon about three. He was in a pitiful condition. He couldn't speak coherently. I left him with Mrs. Coggins —she's the cook—and after about an hour she came down and said he wanted to speak to me, so I went up. He told me about Gates's not showing up. Then I called you."

"That's the boy?"

"Yes."

Smith was lying on a white iron bed in what Bull gathered was a servant's room on the third floor. He was the most fragile person the Inspector had ever seen. The thin transparent hands moved nervously with long twitching fingers over the eiderdown. Mrs. Colton went to his side and took one of the restless hands in hers. Bull felt that Death sat on the other side, holding the other hand. His was the stronger hold.

The old man opened his sunken eyes. His dry blue lips moved without a sound.

"Send for a doctor, Mrs. Colton," Bull said quietly.

She turned frightened eyes on him and nodded. Bull took her place and put his fingers on the fading, fluttering pulse. He shook his head involuntarily. Sitting there alone he felt the thin thread of the old man's life stop and flutter again. He thought of the spool on his mother's sewing machine that he used to watch when he was a child. It whirled evenly as long as the spool was full. When the cotton was almost used, and the pull from the moving foot was too great for the reserve, it jumped and slipped and made uneven stitches. Bull watched the old man. Death on the other side was pulling too hard. There was no reserve.

"That's like life," Inspector Bull said seriously.

He heard people coming up the stairs.

It was Mrs. Colton, her step-daughter Agatha, and a doctor.

The doctor nodded to Bull, who stepped aside. The two women stood at the foot of the bed. Bull found himself watching them instead of the old man. They were both young. One was tall and fair, calm yet radiant as crystal. The other was short and dark, tense, and as burning as some elemental flame.

The doctor straightened up and replaced his hypodermic needle in his bag. He watched his patient with a professional narrowing of the eye.

39

"Pretty far gone," he said to Bull. "Mrs. Colton says you wanted him to talk."

Bull nodded. The frail wraith on the bed stirred feebly and opened his eyes. The lips moved. Bull quickly bent over him. Screened in his great palm, directly in the old man's view but invisible to the three other people, was a small gold key.

He could not tell if the dying man saw it.

The lips moved feebly again. "Gates . . . gone . . ."

The old man's eyes suddenly dilated with fear. He was staring straight ahead of him, at the two women at the foot of the bed. Bull turned suddenly. All he saw was a flicker in two dark eyes, and a tightening of two full red lips. Agatha Colton smiled and put her hands behind her back.

The doctor felt the old man's pulse.

"That's all," he said. "I gave him a stiff dose. Heart too weak. I'll make out the certificate."

Inspector Bull and the two women stood motionless. Everything seemed to have stopped in the room.

Suddenly Agatha Colton turned to her stepmother and said in a voice that was as deadly calm as sunshine over a volcano, "I'm sorry, Louise. I can't stick it any longer. I'm going. Good-bye."

She went out of the room and the three of them watched her without a word.

Bull turned to her stepmother. She was standing with one white hand resting helplessly on the iron bedstead. He had the queer feeling that something terrible had happened without knowing what it was or how to go about it to find out.

The doctor looked from one to the other of them, then back at the door through which Agatha Colton had walked; shrugged his shoulders, and prepared to fill out the death certificate.

CHAPTER TEN

Mrs. Colton turned to Inspector Bull.

"I think I'll go to my room," she said with an obvious effort to keep her voice steady.

"I should, Mrs. Colton," remarked the doctor curtly. "I'll leave you a bromide. I think you need some rest."

It hadn't occurred to Bull that Mrs. Colton and the doctor knew each other. He looked at him with more interest now that he did know.

"Are you the Coltons' physician?" Bull asked when Mrs. Colton had gone down.

"I attend Mrs. Colton. My name's Bellamy. I've known her a good many years. Her brother and I were at school together."

"Did you know Mr. Colton well?"

"I did not," said Dr. Bellamy flatly. "I understood that he preferred to have Nelson attend the family and that he and Mrs. Colton had several arguments about my coming here."

"Why?" said Inspector Bull politely.

"The usual thing, I suppose. He was a jealous fellow. That girl comes by her temper naturally."

"Miss Colton?"

"Yes. I don't think she's entirely to blame. I think she's done everything she could to get along with her stepmother. But it's been difficult. They're about the same age—Agatha Colton is twenty-five and Mrs. Colton twenty-eight—and they're both as temperamental as colts."

"You mean they don't get along?"

"Just what I'm trying to say. You saw the scene a few minutes ago, or I wouldn't have mentioned it. In fact, somebody ought to take the girl in hand until this mess about her father is cleared up."

Inspector Bull gave him a mildly inquisitive look.

The doctor shrugged his shoulders. "If you don't know, let it go at that."

"Mrs. Colton was unhappy with her husband?"

Again the doctor shrugged his heavy shoulders.

"Not more so than most married people I know."

Bull disliked cynicism, was himself most happily married, and was annoyed.

"You're not married yourself, then?"

"No. I see too much of other people's affairs. However, Louise Colton has got on well enough. If Agatha had lived somewhere else I think she and Colton would have managed very nicely. But Agatha was opposed to her father's marrying again. Her own mother had been dead only a year. I fancy old Colton wasn't as suave at home as he was to his duchesses over the counter."

"Was Agatha Colton jealous of her stepmother?"

"Jealous or resentful, one. They tried to hit it off. Agatha wanted to live by herself, take a flat somewhere, but the old fellow was opposed. The two agreed they'd be friendly enough if they didn't have to live together. Colton was a pious, headstrong old ass. Said they ought to love one another."

Bull noticed that the doctor spoke quite without bitterness. It seemed reasonable enough.

"Miss Colton looks as if she had a will of her own. Why didn't she go anyway?"

"No money. Colton never gave her an allowance. She had to ask for every cent she got. As a matter of fact I think she was trying for a post somewhere."

"Did she dislike her father?"

"No, indeed. They got on. At least before his second marriage. I think things are different now—or were."

"What did she mean when she said she couldn't stick it any longer, do you think?"

The doctor shrugged again as he took up his bag.

"Just what she said, I imagine. Unless she's gone already she's probably downstairs—why don't you ask her?"

"Thanks," said Inspector Bull. "I will."

He heard voices in the library and tapped on the door.

Agatha Colton opened it. She was dressed for the street, in a short dark fur jacket and small black hat off her forehead. Her face was white and her eyes had a strained bright look in them.

"Come in, Inspector Bull," she said, her voice tensely calm. "This is Mr. Field, my father's solicitor."

Bull saw a slender, middle-aged man with sandy hair.

"Inspector, I'm trying to persuade Miss Colton not to be precipitate here."

The solicitor smiled at the girl in a half-serious, half-amused perturbation.

"Oh, I'm not being precipitate," she cried. "I've stood it as long as I can. I can't stand it any longer, I tell you."

"Now, my dear. Think of your father. Think how it will look!"

Miss Colton's eyes flashed.

"You make me sick, John Field. What do I care how it looks? Father's dead and I'm going. Do you hear? Going!"

Mr. Field stepped backwards with a gesture of resignation, and bowed politely.

Inspector Bull said, "I quite understand your feeling, Miss Colton."

The quiet authority in his voice brought her to instant attention.

"I'm quite sure you don't," she said sharply. "How could you? You can't possibly."

"Perhaps not, then, Miss Colton. But I do know this. If you leave now you'll be making it harder for everybody, including yourself."

"What do you mean?"

Mr. Field glanced up quickly from the papers he had been taking from his despatch case.

"I mean," said Bull soberly, "that there are several points in connection with Mr. Colton's death that have to be cleared up, and that haven't been so far. And that until then we prefer to be in touch with . . . everybody."

He was watching the girl closely. He saw the gradual dawning of horror in her dark eyes. She turned slowly to the solicitor, who stood by the table, his face blank with amazement.

"Then they *did* do it!" she cried suddenly, in a hard choked voice. "They *did* kill him!"

It was Bull's turn to be horrified.

"Who did?" he said.

She looked at him wide-eyed for a moment.

"Nothing, Inspector. I didn't mean anything."

"Who do you think killed your father, Miss Colton?" Suddenly she laughed wildly.

"Who, indeed? Who do *you* think? Don't be funny, Inspector. Oh, I'll stay. Ring the bell please, somebody; tell the girl to unpack my bag."

She sat down in a big leather chair by the fire and pulled off her hat. She was quite calm again, and stared into the fire, twirling her little hat round and round in her hands. Once she missed it and it fell on the floor. She made no move to pick it up. At last she stood up.

"I'm going upstairs. If you'd like to see Louise, Mr. Field, I'll tell her you're here . . . if the doctor's left yet."

"Thank you. I can wait if necessary.—A very difficult young woman, Inspector."

Inspector Bull wiped his forehead with a fine tan handkerchief. "I'm beginning to believe it," he said.

Mr. John Field was one of those men who while he was at Cambridge was felt a certainty to make a brilliant marriage and some day be Prime Minister. Unfortunately he was lazy. At forty he was still a solicitor with chambers in Gray's Inn. However, he was a successful solicitor. He overcame his laziness enough to build up a fairly lucrative practice, largely for the reason that of the two evils, work and poverty, poverty was the worse.

George Colton was one of his best clients. His business was not large. It brought in only some few hundred pounds a year. But it took almost no time and practically no energy, and as such it was John Field's favourite. Further, it was rumoured

43

—and Mr. Colton had been pleased to confirm the rumours —that Mr. Field was interested in Agatha Colton. Mr. Colton was pleased. John Field certainly spent a good deal of time in the house in Cadogan-square, and if Agatha Colton did not seem to return his interest with as much ardour as her father would have liked, George Colton was not the man to let his daughter's whims stand in the way of her own good.

Bull, of course, was entirely unaware of this. What he saw was an immaculately clad gentleman with slate-blue eyes and sandy hair that was neither as thick as Inspector Bull's own tawny mane nor as thin as Agatha Colton said it was when she wished to annoy her father.

"Miss Colton says that Smith died a bit ago," Field said, with very little apparent concern, Bull thought. "That's awkward. He knew more about Mr. Colton's actual business than anyone."

"Yes, it's too bad," Bull rejoined briefly. "Doctor said the shock was too much. Was he very much attached to Mr. Colton?"

The solicitor hesitated a moment.

"In a sense," he said. "I mean he'd been with Colton's father. I suppose altogether he'd been with the firm half a century, perhaps. Of coure, you know that Mr. Colton was not precisely a 'loveable' man. I mean I should doubt very strongly if there was any deep personal attachment there."

"Well," said Bull. "Why the shock, in that case?"

Again Mr. Field hesitated.

"Well, of course, Inspector," he replied, with a deprecatory gesture, "I wonder if it isn't a mistake to assume that the shock was Mr. Colton's death. After all, Mr. Colton was killed yesterday. Of course, perhaps it was that. I've no way of telling. It's absurd for me to express an opinion."

Inspector Bull decided to waive the point.

"You do know, however, what disposition Mr. Colton made of his property. Was he a very wealthy man?"

Mr. Field took a paper from his pocket.

"The will is quite a long document," he said. "I've jotted down the important points of it here for you."

Bull took the sheet of paper.

"You'll observe," Field said, "that he's left Mrs. Colton his business. He wished it carried on as long as Smith lived. At Smith's death, he suggests, Mrs. Colton should arrange for its liquidation; however, that's entirely at her discretion. He leaves his daughter the income from a block of stocks. That's approximately £1,000 a year. Also a cottage in Surrey. Then there are minor bequests. Smith gets—was to get

—£200 a year for life. Gates £100 for life. Then the residue, which amounts to something like £150,000 goes to his wife."

"Then Mrs. Colton is comparatively a very wealthy woman."

Mr. Field raised his sandy eyebrows.

"No wealthier, Inspector, than she was a couple of days ago, really. Mr. Colton was extremely generous."

"With his wife—but not his daughter, I understand."

"That I know nothing about," Mr. Field said with a smile.

CHAPTER ELEVEN

Inspector Bull had the feeling that crime would be much simpler if women were kept out of it. He viewed female encroachment in all branches of life as deplorable in the extreme. His general attitude was that no good could come of it, and to prove his point he told the story of a friend of his who asked a Metropolitan policewoman at Trafalgar-square the way to Adelphi and was misdirected. The Navy and the street-cleaning department were the only branches of human activity that were free of them. He often thought of joining the Navy for that reason. He didn't because he was always seasick when he made the channel crossing and his wife never was.

Bull felt that his present case would be much simpler if it weren't swirling around the complicated mental and emotional states of Agatha and Louise Colton. Still, viewing his job objectively, he was forced to admit that it it weren't for women there wouldn't be crime at all, and Scotland Yard would have to close shop.

As a matter of fact the thing that annoyed him was not the presence of the two women in the case, but his own apparent inability to place them properly. He felt that they were in it, even that they might be the mainspring of it, but he had no very clear idea why or how. So Bull set out from the house in Cadogan-square and ate a solitary and rather gloomy dinner at Simpson's in the Strand before he went back to the Embankment. He was polishing off some fine old Stilton and washing it down with a pint of bitter when he remembered that he had a guest at home. He wondered how Mr. Pinkerton was managing with the cold mutton; and would the custard be as watery as usual?

Dismissing Mr. Pinkerton and his troubles for the time being, he came out into the Strand and took his way leisurely towards Trafalgar-square. He was well fed; his attitude towards the whole world was much more comfortable. He even greeted a policewoman standing in front of the Corner House, and agreed so pleasantly with Larry Hodder—well known to both of them as an only moderately successful pickpocket—that it was a fine evening, that Larry looked after him with deep suspicion.

Inspector Bull glanced up at Charles I as he turned down Whitehall. He always did. It was a sort of ritual. It was at the feet of Charles I that Bull had won his spurs. He had learned, by his usual patient inquiries and curious imagination, a strange thing about Marcel Dashiel; and one day Marcel Dashiel, wearing the white rose of the Stuarts, came out of a wise retirement long enough to join in the pilgrimage to the statue of the martyred monarch. Inspector Bull was there. Dashiel did not lose his head, but he had the rest of his life in Dartmoor to think over his error.

In his little room Bull got out some paper and a trick fountain pen and cork screw combination that someone had sold him, and tried to make a few notes. Abandoning the pen for a tuppenny stub from Straker's he got on better, and in a short time had before him a sound précis of what he had learned and thought in the course of the day. He folded it carefully and put it in his note-case for further reference. Then he took up the telephone.

"Williams, is Brindley around? Send him up."

"I want the low-down on three people," he said when the young man appeared. "Gates. Lives in Shepherd's Bush. Here's the address. Go slow. I want to know where he is, first of all, and then anything else you can find out. Do that tonight if you can. Tomorrow, get a line on Michael Royce. High-street, Windsor. Here's his address. Don't bother the Midland Bank people there, by the way; I'll see them myself. Then . . . I guess that's all; just the two. Be careful about Royce. Oh, will you tell Severn I want a man to trail Mrs. Colton's chauffeur, name of Peskett. Until I call him off. He lives over their garage. 'Night."

It did not occur to Bull at the time that although he had the gravest doubts about the women in the case he had carefully avoided any check of their movements.

Albert Steiner was waiting for Bull in his flat in Queen's-gate.

"Smedley, of the Continental, is quite alarmed," he said, peering at Bull through his heavy lenses, and smiling tran-

46

quilly at some sly joke of his own. "He seems to think he told you too much."

"If he did I missed it," Bull said. "He told me Mrs. Royce's diamonds were not worth what they were insured for." He decided that it was reasonable to come into the open with Steiner.

"That's quite true."

"What *is* their value, then?"

Mr. Steiner shrugged.

"How should I tell? I've not seen them in twenty-five years. They were worth £35,000 then. But not today. Maybe fifteen, maybe twelve, maybe ten. I can't say. I've not seen them."

"But they're not worth thirty-five? You couldn't sell them for that?"

"No, no. I don't even know that you could sell them. Things are dull."

"Mrs. Colton said she understood her husband had a purchaser. She thought an American. She thinks that is why her husband was bringing them from Windsor."

"It may be so. I didn't know it. Colton mentioned no client to me."

"Why did the insurance company, then, decide at this time to have a reappraisal?"

Mr. Steiner hesitated.

"That is what worries Smedley," he said, tapping the chair arm rhythmically with the tips of his blunt fingers and smiling faintly.

"What do you mean?" said Bull, watching him with his mild blue eyes.

"He says the first move for a reappraisal came from Colton."

The thick lenses played curious tricks with the expert's eyes. All Bull was sure of was that they were watching him, shrewdly calculating; that there was meaning behind their deep calm. It suddenly occurred to him to wonder if Steiner was mixed up in this business.

"What would be his interest?" Bull decided to go more cautiously.

"I couldn't say, Inspector. It might depend on many things. If he had a client—as Mrs. Colton thinks, you say—he would want an opinion. He knew, of course, that the stones would not bring £35,000—at least not from an informed person. He spoke of it at lunch last month, using the case as an example of how estates have diminished."

47

Inspector Bull thought for a moment.

"Did he say Mrs. Royce wanted to sell?"

"No, no. I asked him if she wanted to. There are one or two fine stones in the collection. I might have been interested. He said he thought not."

Mr. Steiner looked out of the window a moment before continuing in his low rich voice with its curious timbre.

"I remember it quite well. Mr. Colton did not think much of them, you see. He said, in fact, that it was a pity someone had not stolen them. I think he didn't like diamonds—if you can understand that. I can. An emerald that he would buy any time or place. I fancy you'll find Mrs. Colton never wears diamonds."

"He said that?"

"As a joke, Inspector. I assure you it was nothing more than that. It was quite natural."

Inspector Bull's face undoubtedly showed his doubt. Mr. Steiner peered at him. Again Bull began to wonder.

"It was merely a joke. I suppose all of us thought what he put into words, Inspector. It's the obvious reaction."

"All of us? Was anyone else present?"

There was no change in Bull's impassive face, but he was watching the thick lenses carefully.

"Let me see. There was Colton and myself, Smedley, and young Royce. That was all."

"Royce was there?"

"Yes. He had come in to see Colton about something, and Colton brought him along. Colton and I were arranging the insurance on the benefit exhibition of Queen Anne plate at Sir Philip Orton's."

"What did Royce say?"

"Oh, he laughed and said, 'No such luck,' or something of the sort. He said if anyone was clever enough to lay hands on anything of his mother's he ought to get the insurance himself."

Bull thought it over. Then he said cautiously, "Did it occur to you at the time that Colton might have given him an idea that . . ."

"That would be difficult to live with?"

Bull nodded.

"No. I'd forgot the incident entirely, until I saw the *Times* this morning."

"Well, Mr. Steiner, I have to keep coming back to this: you can't tell me if Colton had a purchaser?"

"No," said Mr. Steiner. "He didn't say so to me. Colton

was close-mouthed. And in fact I can't imagine him telling his wife. He might have told Smith. You've seen him?"

"Smith died this afternoon."

Steiner looked up with genuine surprise.

"You don't say, Inspector." The blunt fingers tapped on the chair arm. "I saw him yesterday morning. He came to me to see some stones I'd just got from Holland."

It was Bull's turn to be surprised.

"Smith?"

Steiner nodded.

"Smith knows—knew—more about diamonds than any man in London," he said deliberately. "More than I do—much more than Colton did. I'm sorry he's gone. Maybe it was best. Heart?"

"Yes."

There was a moment's silence.

"You don't know Smith's story, I suppose," Steiner said. "He was unfortunate. His father was a jeweller, a partner in Tait and Robinson. They were one of the best firms, thirty years ago. Smith's name was Tait. He got involved with Daisy du Val in 1887 or so. She led a merry chase, Inspector. He was madly in love with her, she was insatiable. The upshot was that he misappropriated various valuables. His father disowned him and the firm prosecuted. Smith was sent away for ten years. When he got out he was thirty-four. Colton's father was a friend of his mother and took him in as 'Smith.' Then Colton kept him on. It was profitable to him."

Mr. Steiner smiled. Bull was fascinated by the quiet dark calm of the man.

"Smith told me only a month or so ago that he got forty-five shillings a week, Inspector."

Bull was a mattter-of-fact man.

"Did Smith know Colton was bringing the stones from Windsor last night?" he said placidly.

"Oh, yes. We talked about them yesterday morning. He said he was anxious to see them. There was a pendant that old Mrs. Royce bought from Daisy when she went bankrupt. And now I come to think of it . . ."

The heavy lenses seemed to look earnestly at Inspector Bull.

"Do you think that could have been one of the stones he did his ten years for, Inspector?"

CHAPTER TWELVE

Mr. Pinkerton was waiting up for his host. He had spent the day thinking very hard, and he was ready with some rather startling conclusions. He was not prepared, however, for a haggard and very tired Inspector of the Criminal Investigation Department who barged in at half past eleven with no interest in anything except a hot bath and a soft bed. Mr. Pinkerton, disappointed, was by very nature mild, inoffensive and patient; he tucked his surmises away in his neat grey little mind, prepared to wait until Inspector Bull was in a receptive mood—probably at breakfast. But by the time Mr. Pinkerton heard the maid's tap at the door and her "Hot water, sir," Inspector Bull was well on his way to Windsor.

For a moment, it is true, the Inspector, stirring his steaming tea and expanding pleasantly with the consumption of juicy sausages and well-cooked eggs at the White Horse Hotel, felt a qualm at the idea of his guest's eating still another lonely meal of Crissie's manufacture. But by the time he had finished his toast and marmalade, and drained his last cup of heady tea, he had forgot Mr. Pinkerton entirely. He was thinking about Mrs. Colton, and about the story Albert Steiner had told him the night before.

Bull left his car in front of the White Horse and walked up the High-street under the towering grey walls of the Castle, past the statue of Queen Victoria, past the building that Wren had built for Anna Regina. He knocked on Mrs. Royce's front door. It was just half past nine.

Mrs. Royce was down. Her tall hat stood on the marble-topped table in the hall. Beside it, somewhat belligerently, lay her black kid gloves, her fur, her beaded bag and her walking stick. It occurred to Inspector Bull at once that Mrs. Royce was going out.

"Good morning, Inspector."

Bull had listened to Mrs. Royce before, but he was unprepared at the moment for her deep vigorous voice. Well fortified, however, with tea and sausage, he felt himself a match for the strongest.

"Good morning, Mrs. Royce." He also greeted her son, who seemed to be steadily, Bull thought, in the position of rear guard. In spite of his mother's command, "Step out, Michael—don't *always* stand behind me!" he seemed, Bull noticed, to manage always to retain such a position. Michael

50

Royce returned the Inspector's greeting politely, but Bull noticed he still had a flicker of amusement somewhere about his face. Bull could not tell whether it was in the eyes or the lips. Personally, Bull could see nothing even remotely amusing in the situation, and he had that vague uncomfortable feeling that serious-minded people have when they meet someone not serious-minded. He thought Michael Royce was making fun of him—not of Humphrey Bull personally, of course, because his own identity was submerged when he was on duty—but of Inspector Bull as investigator of the Royce diamond robbery and the incidental killing of George Colton.

Mrs. Royce fixed an accusing eye on him.

"I've been summonsed, Inspector, to give evidence at the coroner's inquiry this morning."

"That was necessary, ma'am. I hope it doesn't inconvenience you too much."

"Inconvenience indeed. It's not the slightest inconvenience. I always do my duty; and I consider this my duty—to my friend Colton, as well as to Society."

"Oh," said Bull. He glanced at once at young Royce. From the slight elevation of that young man's right eyebrow he gathered that his mother's patriotic and moral sentiment left him unmoved.

"If the inquest is at ten-thirty, Mother, don't you think we ought to be getting on with it?"

"It's at Slough, Michael—don't be asinine."

"I know it's at Slough, Mother. But inasmuch as you don't care to do more than twenty an hour . . ."

Michael Royce received so truly savage a glance from the wicked old eyes, so ferocious a shake of the grizzled old head, that Inspector Bull, seeing him stand his ground, realised that after all he was a man of some parts.

"None of your lip, young man. If you mean that I don't care to fly around the country-side as if a legion of demons were after me, the way you do, then you're quite right. I travel at twenty-five miles an hour; and that's fast enough for anybody."

"Quite so, Mother." Royce's agreement was entirely equable. "All I say is that that being the case, it's just as well to count on it. Give yourself plenty of time—that sort of thing."

From Mrs. Royce's glance at her son Bull gathered that he was not the only one who was not sure that his attitude was entirely serious.

"Very well, then. I'm ready. Tell that girl to bring my hat.

And you, Inspector, are you going along now? Will you come with us?"

"I shan't go just yet, ma'am. I have a number of things to do first. And I wanted to find out from you this morning the exact reason Mr. Colton was taking your jewels to town that night."

"The *exact* reason, Inspector? Has anybody given you an *inexact* reason?"

"Well, there are two theories, ma'am," Bull said politely. "One that you wished to sell them, and that Mr. Colton had found a purchaser. The other, that at the suggestion of your insurance people you were sending them to town for reappraisal."

At first Inspector Bull thought Mrs. Royce was going to have a stroke of apoplexy. He watched the effect of his simple words in dismay. When she spoke, however, she was surprisingly calm.

"I'm sure, Inspector, I don't know what you mean. I had no intention whatever of selling those diamonds. My husband left them to me. I'd be stark raving crazy to think of it. They wouldn't have brought £10,000 on the open market. Anyway, my income is quite adequate—thank you—for my needs. I can't imagine where such a ridiculous rumour started. Can you, Michael?"

"Can't imagine, unless it was Colton," said her son laconically. "Remember he tried to get you to sell."

"As you did too, young man. Both you and Colton thought I was a stubborn old idiot. If I remember correctly that was your attitude."

"Now, Mother . . ."

"Don't 'Mother' me, Michael. I'm quite old enough to know my own mind and what's more I'm just as sane as I ever was."

The question of just how much that meant came into Bull's mind. But Mrs. Royce continued.

"As to that other business, I'm sure I don't know where you got that idea. It's true the insurance people thought the jewels were over-valued. Which I'm quite well aware of. The manager suggested I have them reappraised, to lower my rates. George Colton thought it was absurd for me to be paying insurance on £35,000 worth of jewelry when I had £15,000 at the most. And so did I."

"Then you were quite willing to change the insured value?"

"Willing, young man? I was delighted. You don't get insurance for nothing, I can tell you. For twenty-three years I've paid that wretched company £125 a year. In all that time those diamonds have been out twice. I have no use for them as ornaments, and until my son marries, and marries a woman that won't look like a music hall actress decked out in them, no one will wear them. Now George Colton wanted them appraised by that man Steiner. Why, I don't know. I was perfectly willing to take £15,000 as their value. He was as stubborn as a mule. Now if you want my opinion, Inspector—and I'm sure I don't know why you haven't asked me for it —*I* believe there was another reason for George Colton's taking those stones."

Bull looked at her in the greatest surprise, which he tried to conceal. He was pleased to observe that her son made no attempt to conceal his feelings.

"What do you mean, Mother?"

"You needn't look at me, either of you, as if I'd taken leave of my senses. If you can find out, Inspector Bull, why George Colton took my diamonds to London—with my permission, of course, even if I didn't see the least point in his doing so —then you'll know why he was killed and who did it. We'd better be going, Michael. I'm not driving as if the devil was after me—not if we never get there."

Young Royce pressed out his cigarette in the silver ash tray and helped his mother with her sealskin coat. Bull noticed with the greatest satisfaction that there was no amusement in his dark handsome face.

CHAPTER THIRTEEN

Bull saw Mrs. Royce and her son to their car, a Rolls of respectable years, with a withered-looking man in uniform standing by the door holding a gay plaid rug over his arm like a serviette. When the old lady was properly tucked in, and a stone put at her feet, and the chauffeur had gone for lavender salts and had then returned for a packet of peppermints left on Mrs. Royce's dressing-table, closed the windows so that the car was hermetically sealed, got into the driver's seat and waited patiently until Mrs. Royce was sure she was ready, the car moved off at a discreet lack of speed down the High-street towards Slough.

Bull drew a long breath of relief and lifted the knocker a second time. The butler answered almost at once. Bull knew he had been watching the street from behind the heavy curtains.

53

"I want to talk to you," he said. "We can just step inside; I'm in a hurry."

The man was obviously flustered. Whether he was more flustered than always, Bull did not know. He did know that it would take a stouter heart than the man's frame seemed to indicate to live with Mrs. Royce in anything but a state of perpetual trepidation.

"What's your name?" Bull asked when he had shut the door.

"Murry, sir."

"How long have you been with Mrs. Royce?"

"Thirty-one years, sir."

"Oh," said Inspector Bull. He decided to change his tactics a little.

"You know, of course, Mr. Murry, that Mr. Colton has been murdered."

"Oh, dear, yes."

"And Mrs. Royce's diamonds stolen."

"Yes, sir."

"Did you know he was taking the diamonds to town that night?"

"Yes, I did, Inspector. I heard madam tell Mr. Michael to leave them in her room in a small safe we have, sir. He asked her if she thought it was safe. She said very positively that it was."

Inspector Bull nodded.

"And then I heard them discussing it at dinner, sir."

"They did discuss it, then."

"Oh, yes. Mrs. Colton was opposed to Mr. Colton's taking them. But madam and Mr. Colton assured her it was satisfactory."

"What did Mr. Royce think of it?"

"I don't recall that he made any comment. He doesn't ordinarily, sir."

Was there the slightest hesitation before the "ordinarily"? Bull thought so.

"Why not?" he asked innocently.

Mr. Murry's answer came with explicitness yet dignity.

"You must realise, Inspector," he said seriously, "that we all consider it better for madam to have her own way. The consequences are never so difficult as in attempting to persuade madam to change her views."

"I quite understand. She's a little . . . unreasonable?"

"No, sir—determined, I should call it. I'm sure it would be perfectly possible to convince madam, but it seems much

54

simpler and more . . . peaceful . . . to let her have her own way. I'm speaking, of course, sir, just between the two of us. That's what the master told me when he employed me. He repeated it on his deathbed, sir, and I've always considered him a wise man."

Bull wondered if his wisdom had been shown in dying, but refrained from an impolite question.

"Now, Mr. Murry," he said, "can you tell me this—and it's a very serious matter: was there any mention of Colnbrook that evening?"

The butler's answer came without hesitation.

"Yes, sir. I don't recall how it came up. I went to the pantry, and when I returned I heard Mr. Colton say, 'We go through Colnbrook.' Or something practically like that."

Inspector Bull noted the remote possibility that the suggestion had not come from Mr. Colton.

"Who was in the room at the time?" he went on.

"Madam, Mr. Michael, Mr. and Mrs. Colton. Myself, and Ella. The maid who helps serve."

"Are you sure the maid was in the room?"

"No, sir, I don't remember her actually being in the room. But at dinner afterwards, in the servants' room, I clearly recall her observing that if she were carrying diamonds to London she wouldn't go by way of Colnbrook. Mrs. Thompson, our cook, said, I recall, that she would go that way if she were taking diamonds, because of the two hold-ups on the bypass the week before. I mention that topic only because that was actually what she said, sir."

"Don't mind me," Bull said with a heavy attempt at irony. "You're sure . . . or rather, who was in the servants' room then?"

"Myself, Mrs. Thompson, Ella, MacRae the chauffeur, and Mr. Colton's chauffeur—Mr. Peskett."

"Peskett was there?"

"Oh, yes, sir. I recall that because he said he wished the old boy—as he called Mr. Colton—had told him he was taking the jewels, he'd have brought his pistol. I said that certainly Mr. Colton would be armed. He said then it would be the first time. He said he didn't know whether the old . . . Mr. Colton was not afraid of anything or if he was more afraid of a gun than of being robbed. He said the old . . . Mr. Colton had raised 'what for' once when he told him he had a pistol. After that he had sometimes carried one without telling Mr. Colton."

Thinking all this over, Inspector Bull gave what could only

be described in a man of slighter substance as a grimace. Was there anyone, he wondered, who did not know that jewels were going to town by Colnbrook?

"One thing more, Mr. Murry," he said, "and I'll be getting along. When did the Coltons leave?"

"At about nine o'clock, sir."

"What happened then? I mean, did you see Mrs. Royce again that evening?"

"Yes, sir. I took her her cup of hot Ovaltine at fifteen minutes of eleven. It's one of her rules, sir."

"Where did you take it?"

"To Mrs. Royce, sir."

"Yes; where was Mrs. Royce?"

"In the upstairs drawing room."

"Mr. Royce with her?"

The old man hesitated for a moment.

"Yes, sir."

"He hadn't been out?"

"Not that I know of, sir."

Bull looked at him with a smile.

"You've known Michael Royce a good many years?"

"He was born the year after I came, sir."

"I take it that it was perhaps for his sake that you've stayed here so many years?"

Again the old man hesitated.

"I shouldn't say that, sir. Madam is very kind, even if a little . . . uncertain."

"Nevertheless you wouldn't have stayed on, when you were a younger man, if it hadn't been for the child?"

"Well, sir, perhaps not. Though madam is most generous. She pays me three guineas a week, sir—which I don't think the servants in the Castle can say."

"What I'm getting at, Mr. Murry, is this. If you thought Mr. Royce was involved in this affair, you'd be perfectly willing to lie to save him."

The old man's hands shook a little.

"I think of him more like he was my own son, sir, even if it's absurd for me to say that."

"In other words, he wasn't in when you took Mrs. Royce's Ovaltine up to her?"

"Yes, sir. He was in; but he came in just as I was taking it up. I don't know when he went out, but I saw him come in."

"Did you speak to him?"

"He spoke to me, sir."

"Notice anything unusual about him?"

"Only in a manner of speaking, Inspector," the old man admitted reluctantly.

"What did he do?"

"He didn't *do* anything, sir, except take off his coat and hat and hang them up."

"Well, what was unusual about him, Mr. Murry?"

"It was what he said, sir."

The reluctance was more evident still.

"Yes?" said Inspector Bull, a gleam in his placid eyes.

"Mr. Michael is always polite . . ."

"I know. Yes?"

"Well, Inspector, this night he wasn't. He saw me going upstairs with madam's Ovaltine, and he said, 'Good God, does the old girl still take that ghastly slop?' "

"Oh!" said Bull. "I'll have to be getting along."

The inquest was half over when Bull got to Slough. He sat down next to Holmes of the *Mirror*.

"What's happened?" he whispered.

"Not a damn thing. Old lady savaged the coroner for fifteen minutes. Priceless old girl! That's why he looks as if he'd been in the Turkish bath. Watch him rip everybody else up the back."

Bull glanced around the tiny room. Mrs. Royce was sitting majestically at the side. Her son's chair was a little behind hers. When she spoke to him in her sonorous whisper she had to lean back awkwardly. Once, Bull noticed, her eyes flashed dangerously, and Mr. Michael hitched his chair forward an inch. Bull smiled.

Mrs. Colton in black cloth coat and small tightly fitting black hat was sitting next to her husband's solicitor, John Field. Agatha Colton was evidently not in the room. Peskett was a few seats behind Mrs. Colton and the solicitor. From where Bull sat he had a perfect view of the three groups. Mrs. Colton was the only one who seemed nervous in the least. She kept taking off her gloves and putting them on again, until Mr. Field took them, with a smile, and put them in his pocket. She smiled too and folded her hands over her bag. After that she seemed quieter.

The coroner consulted the papers in front of him. Bull saw Field whisper something to Mrs. Colton and give her back her gloves. She put them on again.

"Mrs. Colton, please," said the coroner. She went to the stand.

"Let me express my sympathy, Mrs. Colton," he said

57

quietly. "We realise that this is a difficult position for you. Will you tell us just what happened the other night?"

Mrs. Colton was pale but composed in face of the crowd of sensation-seekers that filled the benches, craning their necks, commenting on her clothes, nodding at each other knowingly.

"No good can come of that sort of thing," whispered a middle-aged woman behind the Inspector. "She's the one as did it, you mark me!" returned her neighbour. The coroner rapped for order.

"You'd 'a thought she'd 'a wore some jewelry!" the first woman managed to get in before the sound of the gavel died away.

Mrs. Colton told her story directly and calmly. Her composure seemed to strike the audience, which listened in a respectful silence.

When she had finished her story of the actual murder Bull hastily wrote a few lines on a piece of paper, handed it to the bailiff and motioned towards the coroner. The man took it forward. The coroner stopped shuffling among his papers, read it, and glanced over at Inspector Bull. There was a general craning of necks in Bull's direction.

"That will be all, Mrs. Colton. Oliver Peskett, please."

The chauffeur was a better bid for public sympathy. Everyone knew, or so the general atmosphere managed to suggest, that his position was not of his own making, and that he had been, to the extent of his being involved, an innocent pawn of fate. He was quite good looking, and unmarried, or so he testified.

He repeated Mrs. Colton's story. He had not known that the jeweler carried a weapon. He had always believed him opposed to it. He didn't know he had jewels with him until he saw his black bag as he got into the car. No, he had never had any difficulty with his employer. Where was he born? He was born in Puyallup, Washington, U.S.A. No, that was not the District of Columbia; it was in the Northwest. No, it was not in Oregon; it was in Washington. He had joined the British army. Had served in Russia from '16 to '18. Had worked in Birmingham and Manchester. He had thought of taking out papers because he liked the country. No, there was no reason why he didn't go back to the United States except that he didn't want to.

The Inspector thought of sending another note to the coroner, and was about to do so when the coroner dismissed Peskett and proceeded to instruct the jury.

Bull stepped outside without waiting to hear the charge of

wilful murder by a person unknown. He hoped to be able to intercept Mr. Field without making sufficient point of it to attract the gentlemen of the press. People began to come out with the half-holiday, half-funeral air that hangers-on at coroners' courts manage to affect. Suddenly Bull heard a meek voice at his elbow.

"Good morning, Inspector!"

"Pinkerton! Hello, what are you up to here? I didn't see you.'"

"No. I was behind the large lady with the hat."

"Oh. That's Mrs. Royce."

"Yes," said Mr. Pinkerton, with a far-away look in his eye. "That's Mrs. Royce."

CHAPTER FOURTEEN

"Look here," Bull said, taking the little man by the arm and directing him to Mrs. Colton's car, by the open door of which Peskett was already standing. "Go over there and tell Mr. Field that I want to talk to him. Tell him I'll be at Colton's shop at 3.30. Ask him to be there."

Mr. Pinkerton nodded, almost too excited to speak, and Bull turned to the man who had come up and was waiting to speak to him. It was Walters of the *Telescope*.

"Hello, Bull! What'll you give me for the key to the Colnbrook Outrage?"

The reporter grinned at him.

"Anything you like," Inspector Bull said soberly.

"Well, here it is." Walters fished a letter out of a baggy tweed coat pocket and handed it over. "From one of the *Telescope*'s better readers. Only six words misspelled. Riley's all cut up about it. Says we're losing our grip. Beginning to appeal to the lower classes. You know our chart? No words spelled wrong—Cambridge don. Two words wrong—upper middle· class. Six—middle class. Eight—lower class. Ten—Labor M.P. Fifteen—Tory lord. We go in for the eights."

"Let's see it," Bull said.

"Take it along. If you get anything I can use let me know. Want to see Royce before he gets away."

"You know him?"

Walters nodded. He seldom used more words than were necessary until he sat down at his typewriter. Then no one in Fleet-street used more.

"He's a good egg. Cheerio."

Bull dropped Mr. Pinkerton in Piccadilly-circus and drove to New Scotland Yard. He hoped Brindley had got his line on the boy Gates. Not that he felt the boy was materially important, but he would at least solve the riddle of his own disappearance.

There was a note on his desk, re. Gates—James Benjamin, age 51, address Shepherd's Bush-road, occupation jeweller's clerk, unmarried. Left rooms Thursday A.M., not returned. No word. Took black fibre suit-case. Landlady says two shirts, four celluloid collars, one pair socks missing. Other clothes in order. Mr. Brindley was a man of dramatic imagination.

"Landlady reports: 'Quiet, keeps 'imself to 'imself.' Pays promptly. 12/6 a week bed, breakfast and tea. No known relatives, no friends. Only caller an old man, name of Smith. Smith there Wednesday night. Landlady wants to know if he doesn't come back by Saturday can she have his clothes for her husband—he's the same size. I said No!! but she won't wait till Saturday. Have sent out descriptions."

Bull read Mr. Brindley's report without much interest and put it in his file under "Colton." Then he took out the letter Walters had given him.

"Dere Sir," it read, in crude straggling writing, "The police are all rong about , Mister Colton geting murdered. Him and Mrs. fight all the time. She kiled him, her and the driver. Yours truley, a Frend."

Bull read it and put it aside. He was always let down a little, he felt, by anonymous letters, especially letters from servants accusing their employers. This letter he took to come from such a source. The cheap paper, bad ink and pen, together with the knowledge—or claimed knowledge—of the Coltons' private lives—pointed to some one of their servants. Probably the girl who led him outside, Bull thought. He looked at it carefully. Could it be from someone else—Agatha Colton, for instance? He decided that that suspicion was wrong; there was no doubt the letter had been written by an illiterate. The writing was not disguised.

He looked at the postmark. S.W. 5 Earl's-court. That would put the girl—he assumed it was a woman for the reason that it was the sort of thing women did—probably in one of the long deadly streets off Richmond-road. Finborough-road, somewhere along there. He put the letter in his pocket again and smoked a pipe, his forehead screwed into an agony of concentration.

Finally he came to a conclusion and his brow cleared. He reached for the telephone and put in a call.

"Hello, Crissie! Is there a letter for me? From France? Madam's writing? Fine. I'll be home early."

Mr. Field was already at the jeweller's shop in St. Giles-street when Inspector Bull got there at half-past three. He had put up the shutters with the help of the doorman across the way and had removed the black cloth coverings from the show case.

"Mrs. Colton tells me Gates hasn't turned up," he said. "Do you know where he is?"

"I've got a man hunting him," Bull answered. "We've not had any luck so far. Rather holds us up, too. I understand that those two with Colton were the only people who knew anything of the actual working of the shop."

"I'm afraid that's right. Colton was curiously old-fashioned in some ways. I fancy, however, that we can find whatever you want in the papers I've brought along, and the files here. What *do* you want, by the way?"

Field looked up suddenly with an air of perplexity.

"I don't know exactly," Bull said stolidly.

"What I mean is, Inspector, I don't see that anything here is going to help you find out who held up and robbed Colton."

"Perhaps not," returned Bull. "Can you open the safes?"

"No, I can't. I've told you that Colton didn't confide in anyone. He said once that he'd make provisions in case of his death, but he never did, that I know of."

"All right. I've got a man outside who'll open them for us. I wanted you chiefly as a witness."

Mr. Field looked at him in surprise.

"You mean you're going to have these safes forced?"

A faint grin warmed Inspector Bull's simple face.

"No," he said. "Francher won't have to force them. He can open them without any trouble. He's reliable—been working for the Crown one way and another almost all his life."

He didn't bother to explain that at present one of Mr. Fancher's ways of serving the Crown was as cook's assistant at Pentonville.

The man came in, an insignificant, rather apathetic figure with a thin nose and long sensitive fingers. He took off his cap and cast an uncertain glance at the immaculate Mr. Field. He smiled timidly at Inspector Bull.

"That 'er, sir?" he said, nodding at the enormous Davy safe in the corner. "Purty!"

Field put on his pince-nez and looked at the Inspector. He cleared his throat.

"You're quite sure that this is . . . in order?" he asked cautiously.

"You can stop me if you want to," Bull said, "—until I get a court order."

Francher jumped at the word.

"But this is a case of murder, Mr. Field."

"I know it is, Inspector. But I don't see that there's the slightest possibility of finding useful evidence here?"

"Well," Bull said, "Colton's dead. Smith's dead. Gates has disappeared. That's the lot of 'em. They were the only people who could get in this place. Wednesday night, after Colton was shot, a man came here. He came in with a key. Perfectly familiar with the place, do you see? He asked the constable on duty to stop at the door until he came out. Stayed here three or four minutes and went away."

"You think it was Gates?"

"I don't know. Looks like it, doesn't it?"

Mr. Field looked doubtful.

"Nothing was disturbed, Inspector. Look at it!"

He waved his hand around the orderly shop.

"That's just what we don't know, Mr. Field," returned Inspector Bull. "That's what I want to see the inside of these safes for."

The other glanced quickly at him.

"I mean," Bull continued imperturbably, "that if Gates came here knowing what he does about the shop, he could have gone through these safes and emptied them with nobody the wiser until they were opened by due process of law. Meanwhile, he'd have plenty of time to get rid of his haul. That's why I want to see the inside of them—or it's one reason."

Mr. Field said nothing for a moment.

"Mrs. Colton said Smith was trying to tell her something when he came there. Do you think he knew about it? You know his record, of course. Do you think he was involved?"

"And changed his mind when he heard Colton was murdered?"

"Exactly."

Bull shook his head.

"I don't know. Let's see if anything is missing."

"By all means," said Mr. Field.

Bull nodded to the little man, who had drawn a chair in front of the safe and was awaiting orders. He gave the two men a pleased smile and began to work, quickly and deftly.

While Bull watched him—just, he thought, to be on the safe

side—Field began to go through the papers he had in his case.

"This is what we need," he said, handing a sheaf of foolscap to Bull. "It's the inventory. Fortunately, it was taken only three weeks ago or so. Here we are—January 26th."

Bull glanced through the neatly written columns.

"We'll have to have an expert check it before we're through," he remarked. "I suppose we could tell now if there was any considerable tampering."

Francher stopped a moment and leaned back in his chair. He mopped his forehead with a grimy handkerchief and grinned sheepishly at Bull.

" 'Ard work, it is, sir," he said. "I'm a little ahrt of practise, as you might say. An' you cahn't tyke yer time. Yer cahn't never forget yer 'aven't got orl night to it."

He went back to work. In a moment he grinned again as his delicate ear caught the whirr of the mechanism as the bolts slipped into place. In another moment the great door swung open.

CHAPTER FIFTEEN

Mr. Field's troubled face cleared. A faint flicker of amusement disturbed the cold slate blue of his eyes.

"You gave me quite a turn, Inspector," he said pleasantly.

Bull's face seldom showed emotion of any sort. He was one of those fortunate people who feel no responsibility about their theories being infallibly correct. If Mr. Field expected him to be disconcerted when he found the contents of the safe undisturbed, he was wrong. Bull examined the neatly arranged trays of exquisitely mounted stones, and unwrapped several costly ornaments. One diamond and emerald tiara along was worth Bull's income for ten years, even before deducting the tax.

He closed the door of the safe and spun the knobs into place.

Now that one of his theories was apparently disproved, he wasted no time regretting it.

"Will you have the inventory checked within the next few days, Mr. Field," he said. "If there's any motive for Gates's disappearance I'd like to know it. There's no one else that I can see who had a key to the place, and a perfect right to come and go as he pleased."

"Has it occurred to you, Inspector," asked Field, "that he may have come here that night with some perfectly legitimate purpose, and got the wind up when he heard Colton was dead? He must have known, of course, that he himself was one of the few people who knew Colton was bringing the diamonds to town that night."

Bull made no comment. The solicitor continued.

"If Gates had killed Colton and taken the diamonds, he would never have come back here. He'd have taken the next boat to Amsterdam or New York."

"Did he know Colton was bringing the stones in that night, Mr. Field?"

"I should suppose so. It was quite common knowledge. Miss Colton rang me up to try to get her father to send a bonded guard after them in the daytime. As I understood it, Inspector, Mr. Colton had a possible purchaser for them. I see no reason to think Gates wouldn't have known it."

It was time for tea when Inspector Bull and Mr. Field came out of the shop in St. Giles-street, Bond-street. With the aid of the doorman across the way they drew the steel shutters down over the faded emblems of the Coltons' magnificent patrons and locked them.

"I'll run out to Cadogan-square," said Field, getting into his car, "and tell them the place is intact."

He put his foot on the starter.

"May I drop you anywhere?"

"No, thanks," said Bull.

"Very well then, Inspector. I'll take care of the inventory. I'll get two of Steiner's clerks to check it. Do you want to have a man present?"

"I think not. You're an executor? Who's the other?"

"Steiner."

Bull stepped off a bus at the Strand Corner House. It was the most convenient place for tea when he was on his way back to New Scotland Yard. The walk down Whitehall was just enough to cope with the enormous tea of Devonshire cream and raspberry jam that he usually managed to put away.

It was a little after five o'clock when he got a seat by a window on the first floor. He gave the waitress his order and gazed idly around the crowded room. He caught a glimpse of the *Evening Standard* over the shoulder of the woman at the next table. Her husband was reading the back page.

His gaze wandered about. Every paper he could see had

the Colnbrook Outrage inquest displayed in large type. Bull knew what they were all saying. Scotland Yard for all its reputation was unable to cope with simple highway robbery. They were probably citing the case of a recent £10,000 hold-up in an American city—Baltimore, was it?—where the police had got their man in three days. And they weren't Scotland Yard. Bull sighed and poured his tea and stirred it, profoundly comfortable in spite of his critics.

He was finishing his first cup of tea when he saw two people he knew. They came in and took a table not very far from his, on the other side of one the waitresses used for service. They had not seen him, and he was mildly grateful to the stationary young woman whose customers were, for the moment, all fed. She made an effective screen around which he could watch Agatha Colton and Michael Royce without their seeing him.

She was talking softly but urgently. He was listening with far more genuine concern in his handsome dark face than Bull imagined possible. This Michael Royce was very different from the young gentleman with the elevated eyebrow and amused flicker that Bull had seen at Windsor. His face watching the girl was curiously tender.

Bull watched them steadily. The man ordered tea and the girl waited impatiently for the waitress to leave. She continued talking, pushing her plate away with an impatient gesture and leaning forward a little across the table. When tea came, she poured it, handling the tea things with a sort of bewildered delicacy. Gradually she became calmer, and by the time Michael Royce passed his cup again she was smiling.

Detective-Inspector J. Humphrey Bull would have denied, and correctly, any academic knowledge of psychology. But he had a practical working knowledge of how people act. He knew, therefore, from his five minutes' observation, several things. First, that Agatha Colton was not an habitué of Messrs. Lyons' Corner House. Second, that they had just met; because her urgency had gradually subsided. Third, he knew that Michael Royce was in love with Agatha Colton.

Similarly Inspector Bull knew nothing of formal logic. But he knew better perhaps than Aristotle or Whitehead that for some reason Miss Colton and Royce were meeting secretly, that they had chosen this place as the least likely for them to be seen by anyone who knew them. And finally he knew that Agatha was extremely worried about something that Michael Royce had been able to reassure her about.

Bull took the check the waitress pushed significantly in front of him and made his way to the cashier's desk by the door. There was little chance that they would notice him, enormous as he was. They would not have seen an elephant carrying the Shah of Persia. He paid his bill and stepped into the lift. Two women were talking. They wore bright gold wedding rings and had cinema programmes in their hands.

"You needn't to tell me she didn't do it," said one of them indignantly. "It's plain as the nose on your face. She shot him with that revolver. She and the driver."

"There was only one shot from her revolver," said her friend. More, Bull thought, from argumentativeness than conviction.

"Of course! She'd put another shell back in before the police got there!"

It was dark and drizzly in the Strand. Bull turned his collar up around his neck, thrust his hands in his deep overcoat pockets, and turned toward Trafalgar-square. He went slowly down Whitehall, feeling rather depressed.

Brindley had turned in a report on Smith during the afternoon. Bull glanced over it. The man had managed to keep his secret fairly well guarded. There was no mention of the crime that sent him to Dartmoor. In fact there was no mention of anything that would distinguish him from the millions of Londoners who pay their rent, regularly go to business, return home and go to bed. The purple patch in his early life had faded into the distance. He had probably forgot it himself, or thought of it as an adventure in someone else's life. Poor Smith!

Suddenly Bull realised that it was not poor Smith that he was thinking about. It was a man and a girl in a Lyon's tea shop.

He cleared up several minor matters on his desk. Disposed of eight kittens who had started a neighbourhood row near the Oval. Arranged for Piper Tom's aged mother to draw his unemployment insurance while he was at Princetown; and passed on some evidence that connected two cat burglars in Wormwood Scrubs with the erratic Miss Abury of Westminster. Then he got on his hat and coat again.

He went home on the Underground. On the way he read the *Standard* and the *News* over a bank clerk's greenish-black shoulders. He listened to a prosperous-looking draper; he was telling his neighbour that there was no doubt in his mind that Mrs. Colton had murdered her husband.

When he had opened his own front door he saw Mr. Pinkerton sitting in the living room in front of the fire, reading the *Standard*. He turned and tapped the front page significantly with his old-fashioned eyeglasses.

"There's not the least doubt about it, Inspector," Mr. Pinkerton said. "Mrs. Colton murdered her husband."

Bull took off his coat and hat and hung them in the closet. Then he put on a brown velvet smoking jacket and a pair of comfortable house slippers, and sat down on the other side of the fire with his letter from Mrs. Bull.

"I don't believe it," he said, and continued with his own affairs.

CHAPTER SIXTEEN

"I insist Mrs. Colton is the murderer," said Mr. Pinkerton.

They had discussed the case at dinner. Bull had told the little grey man about his interview with the Royces and their servants, and his seeing Agatha and Michael at the Strand Corner House. Then he remembered he had not told Pinkerton what he had done the day before, so he began at the beginning and went over everything again.

"I still insist that Mrs. Colton is the woman."

Dinner was over and they were sitting upstairs in Inspector Bull's dark brown den with the green desk lamp. It was fairly quiet. They could still hear the clatter of pots and pans in the scullery where "that girl"—as Mr. Pinkerton called her—was washing up.

Inspector Bull scowled.

"I don't believe it," he said. "That's what every clerk and shop assistant in London thinks. Go down and ask Crissie. She'll agree with you. I don't."

Pinkerton had never known his friend to be so stubborn before. He took off his eyeglasses and wiped his pale little eyes. Then he polished his glasses and put them on again.

"Maybe you're right, Inspector," he said when he had determined by squinting and examining the title page of a book on the desk that his sight was in order. He looked cautiously at Bull.

"At the same time," the Inspector continued soberly, "there *is* one thing that worries me."

Pinkerton nodded eagerly.

"You mean the motorcycle?"

"How did you guess?"

"I thought of that at once," Pinkerton replied hastily. "It was perfectly simple. There wasn't a sign of a motorcycle in the entrance of that place in the road. And the evening papers said nobody had heard one anywhere on the road at that time."

"In other words," he went on, "there is absolutely no evidence whatsoever—except the word of Mrs. Colton and the chauffeur—that there was a motorcycle, or a man on it."

A troubled frown clouded Bull's simple, ordinarily placid face.

"I've been thinking of that all day," he admitted. "It's a possibility. If it's true it means that Mrs. Colton and the driver are in it together. Then they'll have the jewels stowed away somewhere."

Mr. Pinkerton nodded brightly.

"And in that case, Mrs. Colton just fired her gun as a blind, and the chauffeur had a gun and killed Colton. But what did he do with it?"

Inspector Bull chewed the inside of his right cheek in the deepest meditation.

"That would be easy," he replied. "He could have thrown it over the wall into the undergrowth and got it later. Or he just put it in his pocket—nobody searched him or the car either. They could have put his revolver in the side pocket and put the satchel of jewels under the rug on the floor. I'll just have them search the garden by the wall tomorrow."

He made a note on the pink paper pad on his desk. He had little use for notes. There was no danger of his forgetting even the minor details he was supposed to remember, but if you had a desk you should have pads on it, and if you had pads you should use them if you happened to remember it.

"But if there *was* a man, you've got several possibilities," said Mr. Pinkerton, carefully fitting a cigarette into a long white bone holder and lighting it. "In fact, you've got four distinct possibilities."

"Four?"

"Four."

Inspector Bull's mind was the type that could cope successfully with one possibility at a time. Four were a little overpowering. Not to Mr. Pinkerton, whose agile mind could build edifices that made New York a city of Lilliput. Especially if he had an audience, and Inspector Bull was listening to him with mild wonder in his eyes.

"If there *was* a man," continued the little Welshman with a certain complacent eagerness, "if there *was* a man, four things are true about him.

"First, he knew about the diamonds.

"Second, he knew the car was going by way of Colnbrook —that it was not taking the by-pass.

"Third, he knew the chauffeur didn't carry a gun.

"Fourth, he knew—at least according to Peskett—that if he didn't disguise his voice he'd be recognised.

"Now what does that give us?"

Inspector Bull was making diamonds, squares and circles on his pink pad.

"It gives us," said Mr. Pinkerton, "the four possibilities."

"Four?"

"Four."

"How so?"

"The man and the driver working together," said Mr. Pinkerton; "the man and Mrs. Colton; the man and Mr. Colton; the man and someone not the driver or Mrs. Colton who knew all about it."

Bull gazed at his grey little friend with admiration. Mr. Pinkerton, having built his edifice, wanted no one to tamper with it. He hurried on.

"The man and the driver could have been in it together. From what you said the driver had plenty of time to telephone a confederate—if he wasn't already in the Royce house. He knew Mr. Colton was never armed, and that the driver was not armed. He must have been surprised when Mrs. Colton fired—he lost his head, and fired too. The driver lied about not knowing about the diamonds until he saw the satchel in Mr. Colton's hand, and about not knowing they were going to Colnbrook."

"That's right," Bull agreed cautiously. "In that case the shooting was accidental. If it was Mrs. Colton and the driver it was premeditated. But if it was Mrs. Colton and the murderer, then she wouldn't have fired, would she?"

Pinkerton frowned. He didn't like to appear too positive, however; so he let it go.

"If it were the bandit and Mr. Colton," he began tentatively.

Bull shook his tawny head.

"That means that Colton was trying to steal Mrs. Royce's jewels, and there's no evidence for that."

"There's no evidence against it, on the other hand," Mr. Pinkerton observed judicially. "You don't yet know the real reason for his getting the diamonds."

Bull scowled.

"You don't know but what he may have been in bad shape. Say he got this man Gates to help him put on a robbery. He'd have the diamonds, Mrs. Royce would have £35,000."

They looked at each other.

69

"Suppose it wasn't Gates at all but Michael Royce," said Bull. "Suppose Colton and he arranged it between them. If Royce got £35,000 out of it, and Colton sold the stones re-cut for £10,000, there'd be over £20,000 for each of them."

"At any rate," said Mr. Pinkerton, "it's clear that whoever the man was, if there was one, when Mrs. Colton shot, he thought Colton was double-crossing him. That was the end of Mr. Colton."

They smoked in silence for several minutes.

"That's three," said Bull at last.

"The fourth," Pinkerton said, "is more complicated."

He prodded an infinitesimal stub of Woodbine from the holder, looked at it for some time and eventually decided that it could be thrown away. He remembered that once in Paris, in front of the Deux Magots, an old man picking up one of his stubs from the sidewalk had shaken his fist at him.

He put the long bone holder on the desk and leaned back in his chair.

"The man in league with somebody, not the driver or Mrs. Colton or Mr. Colton, is the fourth."

"It could be Mrs. Royce, who stands to gain £20,000. Michael Royce's interests are presumably the same. It could be Miss Agatha Colton, who apparently doesn't like her father or stepmother."

Bull shook his head.

"She wasn't there. She didn't know they were going through Colnbrook."

Mr. Pinkerton examined his friend's stolid visage critically.

"No?" he said. "You saw her with Michael Royce this afternoon? Couldn't they have done it together?"

"That makes Royce shooting her father!"

Mr. Pinkerton shrugged his shoulders. "It's been done before," he said callously and rather pleased with himself for it.

Bull chewed his moustache, unconvinced.

"It could be Michael and Mrs. Royce, or Michael and Miss Agatha, or Michael and Mrs. Colton."

"Or it could be one of Mrs. Royce's servants without anybody's help."

Bull brightened considerably.

"I thought of that," he said. "That would explain why Peskett would think his voice was disguised but Mrs. Colton wouldn't think of it. He knew him, she didn't."

Mr. Pinkerton smiled with pleasure. His pupil was improving in mental agility.

"Precisely," he said eagerly. "And you can see that that

holds for Gates too. Peskett probably knows him and Mrs. Colton probably has never heard him speak, or barely."

"However," Bull continued, "there's another explanation of that disguised voice."

Mr. Pinkerton decided to allow himself the extravagance of another cigarette.

"There," he said complacently, "are your four possibilities."

"Not four," replied Inspector Bull, switching off the green shaded desk lamp. "Five."

CHAPTER SEVENTEEN

By Tuesday Inspector Bull was no farther along towards a solution of the Colnbrook Outrage than he had been when he and Mr. Pinkerton discussed the matter Saturday evening.

"If there *was* a motorcycle," Bull explained to Commissioner Debenham, "it managed to disappear without a sign."

"How about the old lady in Cranford, Bull?"

Bull grimaced.

"She saw a man with a leather helmet go by about twenty minutes to ten. But the sergeant there says she's a noted liar, sir. He says she's been eyewitness to every misdemeanour within three miles for the last twenty years; when they run her down she was at church or drinking tea in her kitchen. He says she goes to bed at seven-thirty anyway. That's no good, sir. Then the garage man at the London end of the by-pass couldn't remember anybody then."

"What about your other idea? That he turned back towards Windsor at the by-pass."

"He could have done that," Bull said thoughtfully. "He had a furlong or so between the turn and the garage. But even then the garage man ought to have heard him. There's a tobacconist at Slough says he saw three men on motorcycles a little before ten that night when he was going home from his shop. Two of them went through on the Windsor road and the other turned down towards the station. He didn't notice the licence plates of course. But even if we assume that the man came to Slough and boarded the London train—for instance—it doesn't help much. We might still pick that motorcycle up, sir, if he did that."

"What about young Royce? You say the butler saw him come in about eleven?"

Bull nodded.

"He says he went out after cigarettes when the Coltons left. Then he dropped in on some friends in Staines about ten, and stayed there half an hour or so. Had a drink and that sort of thing. I called on them—it's a young Oxford gentleman who has a private printing press and his wife. They say Royce did come, in his car—a racing Hispano —; he comes in often when he's in Windsor. Well, nobody knows about that hour from nine to ten. I didn't want to make a point of it—not yet."

Debenham lighted one of the mild cigars he smoked incessantly, in self-defence, he said, because they were the only form of tobacco his wife and daughter didn't borrow from him.

"Well, Bull," he said patiently, examining the tip of it critically, "you've got to do two things, at least. Find out if there was a motorcycle. Find out who drove it."

Bull allowed himself a grin.

"Sounds simple, sir."

"I know it isn't simple. All we can do is cover the ground. He's getting rope enough now, these few days. He'll do something more. Let him make a mistake and we'll have him."

"I don't want to let him do any more of the same, sir," Bull replied. "And I don't seem to be getting on with it. I was wondering if you didn't want to put Dryden on it . . . He's got a theory. I haven't."

"Bother Dryden's theory. You go find who killed George Colton, Bull, and I'll let you have a week in France."

In his tiny office Bull read two trivial reports from the men who were watching Michael Royce and Mrs. George Colton, put on his hat and coat and went out to Cadogan-square. He reflected as he rang the bell that what he had ahead of him was what he detested most of all parts of his job.

A new maid conducted him into the back parts of the Colton house to the cook, who, he soon found, was in charge of the household management.

"Coggins is my name, or was my husband's name, but it's all I ever got from him but trouble so I call it mine nevertheless. I tell all these girls that comes here no good comes of a girl marrying when she's got a post no matter how bad it is."

Bull sat down and took a cup of tea.

"Do you call this a bad post, Mrs. Coggins?"

("There's what I calls a gentleman. No hoity-toity about him. Drank his tea like my own son, if I'd had one, but Coggins wasn't much good," Mrs. Coggins reported for many a day after the settlement of the Colnbrook Outrage to her cronies gathered at the post office for the payment of weekly insurance.)

"Bad, indeed, sir! The finest post these girls'll ever have. Why the madam is as sweet a lamb as ever drew her breath. And that's saying something."

Inspector Bull agreed. He was fond of old women of whatever social level, unless they reeked of gin too much.

"Now mind you, I don't hold with marrying more than once. I always says that it's tempting Providence. So after I'd slaved, girl and woman, for the Mrs. Colton before her for twenty years and more, it seems a bit hard to have the master up and marry the first pretty face that'll have him. I packs my box ready to leave when she puts her foot in the door. I says to the house-maid as was then, 'No hoity-toity young miss, barely a madam, is telling me her new-fangled thoughts about cooking.' "

In complete agreement, Bull joined Mrs. Coggins in a further cup of tea, strong as witches' brew.

"Tea is tea," said Mrs. Coggins, "and dishwater is dishwater. There's no use using them for purposes God didn't make them for. What was I talking about?"

"Mrs. Colton," said Bull.

"So I was. But no, she no more than gets in this house than she comes straight down here and says, 'Mrs. Coggins, you're a wonderful cook and I'm going to pay you ten pounds a year more, and I wants you to continue just like you've been and wouldn't you like some new curtains for the windows?' As I says to the house-maid, 'Wot could you do?'

"I says, 'Yes, madam,' and unpacks my box and a sweeter body mortal's never had to do for. That was two years Whitsunday and never a cross word."

Mrs. Coggins pursed her lips in admiration and wagged her grey head.

"And if you should ask me, I don't think it's all been roses."

"Ah?" said Inspector Bull between sips.

"Ah. It's not for me to say, but the master, rest his soul, wasn't so jolly as he looked, all pink and shiny and pleasant. Look at the way he's treated that poor lamb his own daughter!"

Bull realised perfectly that no comment was needed.

"Wouldn't let her so much as have young Mr. Royce in the house. Many's the time them two have met here in my kitchen and me standing like the Horse Guards in the pantry

73

till I was ready to drop and the mistress seeing him coming rings the bell so Mr. Royce can get out—and him up at the University too."

"I thought it was Mr. Field who was fond of Miss Colton?" Bull asked with innocence.

"That's according to the master. He was bound and determined that that lamb should marry Mr. Field, but Mr. Field, there's no doubt of it, he gave *his* blessing to Mr. Royce. Those two precious birds have been set on each other since they were in pinafores and longer, and the master was just plain going against Nature. And as I says to the housemaid I'd sooner go against the master than against Nature because you can always get another master and Nature can strike you dead in your tracks. So *I* helps them all I can."

It took Inspector Bull forty-five minutes and seven cups of tea to lead the conversation gently around to the subject of the maid whom he had seen before.

"I gave the worthless baggage the sack," said Mrs. Coggins promptly. "She going around saying—openly, mind you—that the mistress had killed him! The lying little scamp! I always said that girl was no earthly good from the day I hired her. Accusing the mistress of talking to Peskett and Miss Agatha too. I told her Friday night to pack her box and get! And she did."

"Where did she live?" Bull ventured.

"You're not going to listen to any of her talk?"

"Certainly not, Mrs. Coggins. She's been writing letters to the papers. I'm going to tell her to quit it."

Bull saw no reason for avoiding the truth in this instance.

"I just want to stop her before she gets anybody—or herself—into trouble."

Mrs. Coggins got an insurance booklet from her cupboard.

"Well, here it is. 246 Ifield-road. S.W.—I can't make it out. It's out Earl's-court way."

Bull wrote the address in his black note book, for the sake of courtesy; he remembered such things perfectly. It was also a part of his qualifications to need no direction to such roads as Ifield-road.

"Now you're a pretty good judge of people, Mrs. Coggins," he said next. "What about Mr. Peskett?"

"Mr. Peskett's a nice, well-spoken young man," said Mrs. Coggins promptly. "Not that he isn't a bit above himself, because he is. But never a word that's unpleasant from him, and once when the master was away and the mistress said he could he drove me to Haslemere to see my sister and was as nice as you please even to buying me sweet chocolate to eat on the way back. There's not many young men driving people's motor cars that'd do as much. He says, 'Glad to, Mrs. Coggins, you remind me of my aunt that raised me.'"

Scoring one for Mr. Peskett, and marking down another interrogation point for him at the same time, Bull took his way when it was decently possible to Ifield-road. Miss Mabel Gaskin would not have a tongue dipped in motherly kindness as Mrs. Coggins had, but he had some hopes that his interview would not, on the other hand, take so long.

Miss Gaskin gave the impression that she had been waiting some time for a call from the Press but had not expected Detective-Inspector Bull. Bull glanced around the cheap back bedroom with gas ring, shilling metre, chipped basin and pitcher and distorted mirror from Woolworth's over a deal bureau, and modified the severity of his more professional tone.

"I have the letter you wrote to the *Telescope,* Miss Gaskin," he said.

She sat down weakly on the side of her wretched bed. Brazen it out, her voice said; but her eyes were frightened. Bull hated above all to badger servant girls. They had so little but fear to fall back on.

"I guess I've a right to write to papers if I choose."

"You have to be careful about it, though," said Bull, "or you might be guilty of malicious slander."

His voice was gentle, but the words were not pleasant. He hurried on.

"But what I want to find out is this. What did you have in mind when you wrote that? Don't you like Mrs. Colton?"

"I hate the lot of them."

Miss Gaskin might be frightened, but she was not frightened out of her firm beliefs.

"And Mrs. Coggins always being so pleased because the new mistress depended on *her*—all because the new mistress was too lazy to run her own house. She didn't bother about nothing in the kitchen. Paid Mrs. Coggins ten bob a week more instead of hiring a housekeeper. But I wasn't taking any of her fancy talk."

"That's no sign she killed her husband," said Bull sensibly. "A lady can like not to do housework without being a murderess."

That was a little hypocritical of Inspector Bull; of two women, one housewifely and the other not, he would have put money on the second as a possible murderess without a second's thought.

"No, but they fought all the time. Whenever he was home there'd be trouble about something. He didn't like the way she left Mrs. Coggins to run the house. He used to say she spent too much money on clothes and things, he wasn't a millionaire and she'd bankrupt him. And she used to let Mr. Royce come there to see Miss Colton when the master had said she wasn't to. He locked them both in their rooms once. I took their dinner up on a tray. Bread and tea was all he let them have."

Bull listened with inward surprise to this straight-forward tale. It had all the marks of truth as far as it went. If it was true, Bull hadn't a doubt Mrs. Colton had killed her husband. Bull didn't blame her.

The girl was quick enough to see what he was thinking.

"And why shouldn't he, sir?" she demanded, to his further surprise. "It was *his* money, when they had any."

Again she caught his thoughts.

"We had to wait for our wages, once. It was her fault— the fighting, I mean. She knew he'd be set in his ways when she married him. It wasn't *her* place to set herself up against him—no matter what he did. He gave her a home."

Bull would not have been English if he had not had at heart much the same belief.

"Had they quarrelled at all that day he was killed?"

"Rather."

"When?"

"When they were dressing to go to Windsor for dinner."

"What about?"

"Well, I didn't hear it all, but I heard him say if she left the top off the toothpaste again she could leave his house. And stay."

For the first time Bull felt some sympathy for the dead man.

"Was he always cross?"

"No. Sometimes he was lovely, when they pleased him. His wife and daughter. Mostly they'd just set themselves up to provoke him."

"But still, it's quite another thing to say she killed him."

Miss Gaskin's lips set and her eyes gleamed.

"So she and Peskett could go away together. They did it. He's not a driver. He's above that. And she was always as nice as pie to him. Never treated him like a servant."

That, Bull found by careful questioning, was the total reason for Miss Gaskin's belief. As it came out in the course of the questioning that she was out of work he added, to some sound advice about anonymous letters, one of the Crown's

76

pound notes. Of Mrs. Coggins and Miss Gaskin, he thought, one was a much better judge of character than the other. Which it was he had little doubt, though he hated to admit it to himself.

CHAPTER EIGHTEEN

Mr. Oliver Peskett was in his room over the garage that George Colton had built in what had been the side garden of his home. Now and then he looked up from the work he was doing and listened intently. Once he heard steps on the pavement below. He moved quickly from the door and thrust the tools he was working with under his jacket lying on the table. He stepped to the small casement window overlooking the court yard and peered through the curtains. He waited until he saw the retreating figure of the fishmonger's boy, and then went quietly and quickly back to his work. A few minutes later he brushed the fine wood dust from the floor in front of the door leading down into the garage, and put the brace and bit and screw-driver into the drawer of his wardrobe. He washed his hands in the bowl in a corner of the room and put on a grey tweed coat and soft hat.

Oliver Peskett had very much the air of a man who wasn't quite sure in his own mind if everything was, as he would have said, O. K. He examined the small book he had taken from his bureau and put it in his waistcoat pocket. He looked around the room and finally, with something of a devil-may-care shrug of his shoulders, opened the door and went out. He locked it and put the key in his pocket. He went down a few steps, stopped, and with a curious calculating smile at the corners of his mouth came back up the steps and unlocked the door again. He did not go inside; he merely pressed the catch of the Yale lock and closed the door. Then he tried it. He went downstairs still smiling.

When he came out into the street his face was normally serious and he was apparently unconcerned with the possible consequences of leaving his door unlocked for anyone who cared to enter while he was away.

He glanced very naturally down the road before turning up into it. No one was in sight except a postman with his letter sack by the pillar-box on the corner. Peskett kept on. At Sloane-square he entered the Underground and took a ticket to Piccadilly-circus. From Piccadilly-circus he walked by a roundabout way to Covent-garden. At Covent-garden he entered the Tube. He got off at Holborn and took a bus to Tottenham Court-road. At Tottenham Court-road he took a second bus, which he left at Camden-town.

At Camden-town Oliver Peskett, without even a glance around him, walked directly to the Camden-town branch of the Midland Provincial Bank, and deposited a roll of notes which he dragged out of his coat pocket. Not far from him stood a postman who had come in just after him, and who proceeded to engage a young clerk in conversation about the M.C.C. in South Africa. The postman thought the M.C.C. were getting too old. The clerk thought Jack Hobbs could still get his centuries as well as anybody, and could do so even if he had a broken leg. The postman thought nevertheless it was time for the youngsters to have a chance. The clerk demanded, "Where are the youngsters?" At that point Peskett pocketed his pass book and went out; and the postman changed the subject abruptly and asked to see the manager. The clerk looked at him with open mouth.

A harassed manager let his glance fall on the postman's card, and in two minutes Oliver Peskett's account, under the name of Orrin Perkins as it happened, was brought out. In nine days deposits had been made amounting to £300. The sums had been presented invariably in the form of one-pound notes, £50 at a time. The postman picked up the telephone, called New Scotland Yard and gave Inspector Bull the first welcome news he had heard for some days.

Mr. Peskett returned to Cadogan-square by a less circuitous route, went out to the garage, climbed the stairs, opened his door, and stood in the doorway. Inspector Bull sat placidly at the window, smoking a cigarette.

"Good morning, Mr. Peskett," he said. "Thought I'd come around and have a talk with you. Found the door open, so I walked in."

"Morning," said Peskett. He came in and hung his hat up on the back of the door. "Found the old boy's diamonds?"

"Not yet. I thought perhaps you could help me."

The chauffeur grinned amiably.

"Not me," he said.

Bull watched him with mild blue eyes.

"Oh," he said. "I thought you'd be able to. Tell me about the £300 in the Camden bank."

Peskett took the cigarette out of his mouth and stared with badly concealed surprise and chagrin at the Inspector.

"You see," Bull went on, "you've put quite a lot of money away out there. One pound notes always. Now considering

78

what's happened, the Criminal Investigation Department would rather like to know where you got it."

Peskett grinned as amiably as before, and lighted a second cigarette.

"Oh, a gift," he said cheerfully. "A bequest—wealthy old aunt, grandmother, what have you. In fact, Inspector, it's just none of the what-you-may-call-it's business."

"We'll have to make it so, I'm afraid," said Bull as cheerfully. "Now what about it? Better for you in the long run."

The chauffeur was silent for an instant. He stood in the centre of the little room, returning Bull's mild glance with one more calculating than hostile, and not in the least afraid.

"He knows where he stands," Bull thought with a glow of satisfaction. There was nothing he liked better than to have people who had done suspicious things show such confidence. It was a sure sign of several things. Bull felt for the first time that he was getting on with his case. He took out his note book.

"Where did you get the money?"

Peskett shook his head calmly.

"No answer, Chief."

"I'm afraid I'm going to have to arrest you as an unregistered alien," Bull suggested. He tried to get a note of regret in his voice.

The chauffeur laughed a little.

"That's all right with me. That's not stealing diamonds or shooting a fellow. I'd just as soon go back any way."

Bull felt it was very likely. He changed his tactics. Peskett knew as well as he did that so far from putting him out of England it was very necessary to prevent him from going. Get him suspicious, Bull thought; see if he won't do something.

"I didn't say you'd stolen the diamonds," he said calmly. "Or shot Colton either. Where's Gates?"

Peskett seemed both taken aback and surprised.

"Gates?" he said.

"That's right. Gates. Ever heard of him?"

"Sure, I've heard of him. I don't know where the hell he is. He owes me ten quid—hope you find him before you send me off. I'll be needing it."

"I don't see why you need it. You seem to be doing pretty well."

Inspector Bull was rewarded with another pleasant smile.

"Now look here, Inspector," the driver said. "I don't know where Gates is—get it? But if I did I wouldn't tell you. Get

79

that too? I'm not telling you anything you don't know. Now if you'll excuse *me*, you're wasting your time and mine. I've got to take Mrs. Colton to Windsor right after lunch and I'd like to get a bite myself before I start."

Bull got up. A faint twinkle lighted his blue eyes an instant.

"Maybe I am wasting yours," he said, taking his hat. "I'm going to let the registration business go. But you ought to drop in at Bow-street and get a card. Use me as a reference if you like."

"I thought you would, Inspector. Maybe I will."

Bull opened the door.

"Good-bye," he said.

"Good-bye, Inspector. Mind your head. The ceiling's low."

"Thanks," Bull said.

Peskett closed the door and watched the Inspector from behind the curtain. He saw him get into his car and start the engine, shift into second, then into high. He knew the Inspector had gone.

Peskett glanced around the room. He hadn't a doubt it had been searched. He looked around carefully. Nothing seemed to have been disturbed. He smiled and washed his hands before going off to have his lunch with Mrs. Coggins and the new maid in the kitchen.

Inspector Bull, headed for the Embankment, had learned several things. The first and most important was that Peskett, in spite of his sangfroid, was afraid of somebody. He was not afraid of having his room searched, nor was he afraid of some thing. He was afraid, Bull repeated to himself, of somebody. Men with hidden sources of income don't screw brand new bolts on the inside of their door and then go away and leave their door open for anyone to enter if they wish. Wherefore, reasoned Bull, Peskett is afraid of someone who is going to come when he is in his room. Bull wondered if Peskett would be ready—and who somebody was.

At his desk in New Scotland Yard Bull had a moment's conversation with Ames, who had discarded his postman's uniform.

"I want you to keep on watching Peskett," he said. "See who he meets and where, and especially keep an eye on the house and garage when he's there. Tell me who comes. I'm putting on Waring too; I want one of you there always. Try to get in the garage at night if you can."

At the Rainbow in the Strand, over a Lancashire Hot Pot and two pints of bitter, Inspector Bull explained it all to Mr. Pinkerton.

"It's one of two things," he said. "Either the man who held them up is a myth invented by Mrs. Colton and Peskett, and they're running the show between them, or there *was* a man who's in it with Peskett."

Mr. Pinkerton blinked his pale grey eyes.

"And that man is Gates?" he queried.

"Right."

Bull said that more positively than he really felt.

"Where's the money coming from then?"

"From Gates. Gates is selling the diamonds."

Pinkerton took off his small steel-rimmed spectacles and polished them judicially with his serviette.

"Then Gates is selling them in small lots," he said.

Bull looked at him.

"Of course," Mr. Pinkerton repeated complacently. "If he'd got rid of 'em, and got paid all at once, Peskett would jolly well see that he himself got paid all at once. His getting paid in driblets is the surest sign of what Gates is up to."

Bull nodded cautiously.

"But if that's the case, we'd have got a line on Gates. We know most of the fences who'd handle that type of stuff. Nothing's turned up, though."

Pinkerton adjusted his spectacles, took a small sip of his lemon squash, and tested his vision by peering out of the window onto the house roofs, with first one eye closed and then the other.

"The trouble with Scotland Yard," he said at last, with some courage, "is that you're all prejudiced."

Bull waited patiently.

"What I mean is, why look for a fence when you're dealing with actual merchants of precious stones? That's what I mean."

Inspector Bull stared at him in as much astonishment as if Pinkerton had charged that the Archbishop of Canterbury had run off with the canon's vestments.

"You don't mean Mr. Steiner, Pinkerton?" he said, with a frown.

"Well, I'm afraid that's who I did have in mind."

Pinkerton was timid but steadfast.

"Maybe it *is* absurd, but it just occurred to me that he's all mixed up in it, and precious stones do funny things to men. I mean the love of them."

Inspector Bull looked at his friend with some severity. "Nonsense, Pinkerton! It's your chapel training. Here, miss, where's our bill?"

81

He paid the bill and went scowling down the stairs, followed by his little friend.

"I hope I've not . . ."

"That's all right, Pinkerton. Nonsense! Get it out of your head. Cheerio, see you tonight."

Bull patted Mr. Pinkerton on the shoulder, set off across Fleet-street, and turned up Chancery-lane. Passing the premises of Messrs. Studd, Millington, Studd, Millington and Studd he stopped to look at cinnamon brown tweed displayed in the window. But it didn't, strangely enough, really interest or even occupy him.

"Albert Steiner, Albert Steiner, Albert Steiner!" The words kept going crazily through his head. Suddenly he smiled and his eyes fell on the pleased face of a clerk peering through the glass. Bull nodded and went on to Holborn.

CHAPTER NINETEEN

Inspector Bull crossed Holborn, undecided whether to take the Underground at Chancery-lane and attend to a small matter in Knightsbridge, or step around to Hatton-garden to see Albert Steiner then and there.

The memory of his previous talk with Steiner deterred him from the latter course. If the jeweller were involved in any way with the Colton affair, then it was obvious that he had not been entirely frank with Bull that evening in his flat at Queen's-gate. Bull knew his own limitations. If Steiner was not being frank, he, Bull, was no match for the dark enigmatic Jew in a battle of wits. Bull admitted that, while being Nordic enough, however, to feel that given time Scotland Yard would be more than enough for him. Nevertheless he decided to postpone his visit to Steiner until he had a little more to go on.

He had come to the decision and had stepped into the station when a man touched his elbow.

"Sorry, sir—did you drop this?"

Bull glanced at the penny box of matches in the man's hand.

"Thank you," he said, and stepped to one side, by the wall.

"Peskett's out there now," the man said quietly.

Bull nodded and went out. He followed the man and saw him glance to the right as he passed the narrow lane before he continued straight ahead. Bull moved to the corner, keeping near the inside edge of the street, and saw his man.

Peskett, dressed in dark lounge suit, was talking to a middle-aged man of medium size, wearing a bowler hat and obviously ill at ease. Whatever the situation, it was apparent that the chauffeur had the upper hand. The man glanced cautiously to left and right and nodded.

Inspector Bull's bulk and general appearance made it hard for him to shadow a man in even a very crowded thoroughfare. Being perfectly aware of this he crossed the narrow opening of the lane and caught up with Ames, who was examining a fabric trunk on display in front of a leather goods shop a few doors on.

"Who's with him?"

"Don't know, sir. He was waiting there when we came up. They'd been there about two minutes when I spotted you."

"Keep an eye on both of them. Give me a signal when they separate. I'll try to get a line on him. You stick to Peskett. I don't want him to see me."

"There he goes now, sir!"

Bull turned to see the chauffeur cross the street and quickly board a bus that was just pulling out.

"Get on with it!" he said. He went back quickly into the lane.

The man had disappeared.

"Couldn't have had a lot to say," Bull thought. He was mildly annoyed at his miscalculation.

They must have met for some purpose that took very little time to settle. Still it had to be done personally. Did the man have something to give Peskett? Peskett seemed the aggressor. Should he have arrested the man at once? Bull had the uncomfortable feeling that he had made an error in judgment. Had he even gone so far as to let Gates slip through his fingers?

Bull grunted in annoyance and, for want of something better to do, continued up the lane to Jockey's-fields. It then occurred to him for the first time that he was in front of the row of Georgian houses that bound the west side of Gray's Inn, and that, in other words, he was very near the chambers of the Coltons' solicitor, Mr. Field. Bull took out his note book and found the number. 8-A. It was a few doors on towards Theobald's-road. Bull rang the bell and waited.

Bull had no particular reason for seeing Mr. Field at this time. He was more interested in seeing either Mr. Steiner or the man to whom Peskett was talking; and Inspector Bull was a firm believer in the infallibility of coincidence. He regarded it, in part, as a part of the guide system arranged by Providence for the benefit of harassed policemen. Today he had

83

eaten at the Rainbow for the first time in two months. Instead of taking a bus on Fleet-street he had come up Chancery-lane to Holborn. There he had run into Ames on the trail of the chauffeur. Now that he should so come upon Peskett talking to an unknown man almost at Mr. Field's door did not seem miraculous to Inspector Bull, who had often said that if you stood for a year in Piccadilly-circus you would see everyone you had ever known. But still less did it seem meaningless. To have disregarded so obvious a pointing hand would have been, in Inspector Bull's own words—even if millions of other people also used them—"flying in the face of Providence."

So Inspector Bull rang, and rang again, and waited. He heard the shuffling of feet. The door opened.

"Mr. Field is not in, sir."

Bull stepped into the doorway.

"I don't want to see Mr. Field. I want to see you."

He handed the man his card. The hand that took it trembled a little. The man who had been talking to Peskett moistened his lips.

"Will you come this way, sir."

"What's your name?" Bull asked.

"Doaks, sir. Martin Doaks."

"What do you do here?"

"I'm Mr. Field's man."

"How long?"

"A year, sir, and a little over."

"Do you see much of Peskett?"

The man's hesitation was not long, but it was perceptible.

"Peskett, sir?"

"Peskett. Mr. Colton's chauffeur. The man you were just talking with down the lane."

"Yes, sir. I see very little of him, really. Only when Mr. Colton came down here, or to Mr. Field's cottage in Kent."

"Was that often?"

"No, sir."

"Well, what's he up to?"

"Up to, sir?"

"Up to. What was he talking to you about?"

Mr. Doaks's perturbation was not concealed. His face was colourless, his hands shook, he stammered and stumbled in his speech.

"It was nothing, sir."

"Where were you the night Mr. Colton was robbed and murdered?"

"I don't know anything about it, sir, and that's God's

84

truth," he cried. "He said he wouldn't tell, the sneaking hound!"

The terror-stricken vehemence brought an expression of mild dismay to Inspector Bull's placid face. He was astonished at the change in the man. If he had been nervous before—which Bull, knowing the effect of his card on many people who outwardly had nothing to conceal, could readily understand—he was now in the grip of overwhelming terror.

"Now, Mr. Doaks!" Bull said reassuringly. "Pull yourself up. Sit down over there. I want to hear all about this."

Doaks made an effort.

"It's all right, sir," he said with a ghastly smile. "If he told you I was at Slough I had a good reason for being there."

"What was it?" said Bull.

"I was visiting my brother. Wednesday's my day off. That's what I was doing."

"I see. Why didn't you want Peskett to tell me you were at Slough?"

"Because it's near Colnbrook, that's why."

Bull looked curiously at him.

"A lot of places are near Colnbrook, Mr. Doaks," he said. "Your name *is* Doaks, isn't it?"

"That's right, sir."

"Well, what were you and Peskett talking about?"

Doaks had succeeded to a large extent in recovering himself. Here he made a mistake. He took a covert but intelligent glance at the kindly simple face of Inspector Bull, and made the erroneous but natural judgment that Bull was as simple as he looked. It was to that deceptive appearance that Bull owed half his successes.

"I . . . it wasn't anything of importance," Doaks said more calmly. "You're only guessing, Inspector. You don't know anything. Coming in here and saying Peskett double-crossed me!"

Bull shrugged his very large shoulders.

"I don't remember saying that," he said simply. "As I remember it, it was your own idea."

He put on his hat and got up.

"If that's the way you feel about it, it's all right with me," he said amiably. "But I'd be careful if I were you. Doaks, you said the name was. Good day. Don't try to leave town."

Bull went down the stairs leaving Mr. Doaks looking very uncertainly after him.

"Doaks, Doaks, Doaks, Doaks," he muttered. He had heard the name somewhere. "Doaks, Doaks." He racked his brain as he closed the door behind him and started down towards Holborn. Then he smiled. Things were picking up. He remembered. Doaks was one of the names on the list of motorcycle owners in Slough. He had noticed it at the time because when he was a young constable on point duty along the North Woolwich docks there was a public house keeper there named Doaks. One night his wife went off with a sailor from Madagascar and Doaks jumped off into the river. Somebody had made a jingle that began

> *Jolly old Doaks*
> *Jumped off the docks.*

Inspector Bull remembered no more of the lyric, but the name brought back, as he thought of it, memories of cold blowy nights and Mr. Doaks's back parlour after closing time. In spite of Mr. Doaks's sad end it was the bright spot in Inspector Bull's early days on the Force.

Bull thought he could figure it out now. Doaks knew Peskett. Peskett knew Doaks was at Slough and that he had a motorcycle. Assuming that Doaks knew Colton's plans, which he might have done through Peskett, or through snooping in his employer's affairs, or in collusion with someone at the Royces' in Windsor, he could have been at Colnbrook when the Coltons arrived. Assuming that Peskett's first story was true and that he had later recognised Doaks as the man who held them up—then Peskett's bank account and visit to Doaks was explained. Peskett was not accomplice in the crime but accessory after the fact. In other words—blackmail.

Bull lighted a cigarette and made his way slowly and thoughtfully to Holborn, allowing his new hypothesis to grow luxuriantly. At the first tobacconist's he stopped and made a short phone call to Scotland Yard. Then he proceeded methodically along, still engrossed in contemplating the possibilities of Mr. Doaks. There was only one thing against Mr. Doaks as criminal, he thought; but it was a serious fault for a first-rate theory to have. Bull recalled the quivering terrified man at the head of the stairs. It took nerve to hold up a car. It took more to rob a man like George Colton of a satchel full of diamonds and make a quick and precise getaway . . . even if it did not take nerve to shoot a man down in cold blood.

Inspector Bull shook his head. Nevertheless he took a taxi to Paddington and caught the next train for Slough.

CHAPTER TWENTY

Bull settled himself as comfortably as possible in the corner of a third class carriage, and turned the business of Doaks still further over in his mind.

Doaks had got the wind up over something. That much was plain. No one, however, knew how deceptive such states could be better than Bull. In fact the more upset such a man as Doaks was, the clearer it usually was that he had committed not a major crime but some paltry misdemeanour—sold ham after hours, gone through one of the new red lights at Oxford-circus, something of that kind.

Still, the only motorcycle that had turned up in connection with anybody was connected with Doaks. That much was also plain.

Bull could not have told why he was on his way to Slough with a less depressed feeling about the Colnbrook Outrage than he had had the day before. The truth was that he was glad the focus of the case had shifted from the several possible theories that had so relentlessly involved Mrs. Colton. It was preposterous to suppose that she was in league with a person like Doaks. That much of Inspector Bull's faith in appearances was unshakeable. Louise Colton was a beautiful woman. As such it was perfectly possible for her to help kill and rob her husband; that Bull admitted; but she could not be as beautiful as she was and be in league with an inferior creature like Doaks. Or, Bull reflected, Peskett either; although Peskett was not a Doaks by any means, nor an inferior person by any but artificial standards. What Bull meant was that given a desert island with Doaks and Peskett along, Mrs. Colton could find an equal in Peskett but never in John Field's valet.

At Slough Bull went directly to police headquarters and got a young constable to show him the way to the Doaks cottage on the outskirts of the town. It was in a row of bleak and unprepossessing houses.

Mrs. Doaks, an anæmic, harassed woman of forty-five or so, wiped off a chair with her apron and asked Bull to sit down. The constable she knew and was not formal with. Bull decided she had been a house servant in a good place in her youth. He decided also that Mrs. Doaks was on her guard.

"Are you on the phone, Mrs. Doaks?" he asked.

"More's the pity," she replied ungraciously. "My husband's

by rights a contractor, and we have to have it in a business way. Times is so bad we've precious little use for it these days."

"What does Mr. Doaks do now?"

"He's working on the new villas, sir, they're putting up on the London road. Until times pick up a bit."

"Drives to work on the motorcycle, I suppose?"

"Not now he don't. I says to him, a gallon of petrol will buy more than a gallon of milk, and he can walk to his work like other men. The children need it more than he does."

Inspector Bull noticed that her chin was as determined as her brother-in-law's was weak.

"I wonder if I could see it, please."

Mrs. Doaks promptly opened the side door.

"There it is, and welcome. It ain't been used for a month or longer. I put my foot down on that. I drained all the petrol out with my own hands."

Bull went out to the shed, with the constable, and looked at the machine. Then he came back into the house.

"Now, Mrs. Doaks, I understand that your brother-in-law was here a week ago Wednesday?"

"Yes, sir. He comes down mostly, when he has a day off. It's something like home to him, what with the children so fond of him."

"What time did he come?"

"He came just before dinner. He says that Mr. Field, his gentleman, went out to lunch, so he got most of the day off."

"When did he leave, Mrs. Doaks?"

Bull wondered if there was a guarded look in the woman's eyes. Was another of the Doakses hiding something? Bull looked at her almost with impatience. "Why don't they come out with it?" he thought.

"About half past nine, sir. He caught the 10.04 express to Paddington."

"Then he was here until half past nine?"

This time she hesitated palpably.

"Yes, he was. At least, he was with my husband. I went to bed about nine. I have the children, and I have to get up early. My husband was with him."

"Here in the house?"

"No. I think they walked around a bit."

"They took the motorcycle?"

The thin lips closed tightly.

"They didn't have that thing out," she said stubbornly. "I'd have given them what for if they had."

The motorcycle, Bull reflected, with appreciation of the

irony that might be involved, was evidently a bone of contention in the Doaks household. He started another question, when suddenly there was a wild commotion in the front of the house.

"Land's sakes!" said Mrs. Doaks in vexation. More children than Bull would have thought could be attached to one household rushed into the room. Out of the general babble Bull gathered, to his great but guarded interest, that the new parlour suite Uncle George had promised was at that moment arriving.

Mrs. Doaks bit her lip and glanced sharply at Bull. Bull, looking calmly out of the front window, had already observed the gorgeous tan and red and green jacquard davenport coming in the door. It meant, obviously, that Uncle George had come into money in what might be called a big way. A kind-hearted man, he hoped for Mrs. Doaks and the many small Doakses that Uncle George had not been as indiscreet as he thought he had.

"That's a handsome piece, Mrs. Doaks," he remarked, taking his hat. "Good day, and thank you."

"Now take me to the husband," he directed his constable.

The other Doaks was very much like Uncle George, except that he had a narrow pointed face with crafty eyes and a bald head. If guile was not written in that face, it had never been written, Bull thought. He reflected that in case he ever should want contracting done he would remember that Mr. Doaks was not to do it.

Doaks admitted at once that the motorcycle had been out, as Bull had seen at a glance, within the last few days. More, he admitted quite readily that it had been out Wednesday night last when his brother had been at their home. His wife, however, was not to know it, because she wouldn't hear of his wasting money on petrol when times were so hard. Bull could understand how it was. The little woman was hard-working and chapel-going and took care of her home and her children. But she was a little hard on her husband. Moreover, she had an annuity of £75 left by an old lady she had worked for. That made her more positive than her husband liked; but £75 was £75. You couldn't say she was close except in matters of petrol, tobacco and beer.

As a matter of fact Wednesday night his brother George was with them and got a telephone call about eight o'clock. He said it was from his employer, but between men of the world it was a woman. He could hear her voice. He couldn't hear what she said. But when she was through, his brother asked if he could borrow the motorcycle. He was glad to oblige, provided George saw she was filled up before he got home. No, he didn't know where George had gone. He wouldn't care to say if he did. His brother was a hard-working man, and if he liked a drop occasionally, and had a go once in a while with the ladies, it was no more than was natural.

Bull could understand that. He wondered if Mr. Field could.

"Well, thank you, Mr. Doaks," he said. "That's a fine looking piece of furniture your brother sent out today."

The man looked at him sharply. Bull caught the tell-tale glint of fear in his eyes.

"Oh, yes. George is a fine boy. Generous to a fault. Always saving his money, he is, and sending little things to my wife. I tell them it's no use; I'm hale and hearty and good for fifty years, and he'd better get him a wife for himself, to shower his presents on. Good day, Inspector."

Bull smiled in spite of himself. Nevertheless the picture of Mrs. Doaks being showered with presents was a little pathetic. Bull was willing to wager that the red green and gold suite was the first present she had ever got. Since the £75 annuity, of course. He left Mr. Doaks to his work, wondering how much the uneasiness of both man and wife mattered, what it meant, if anything; and particularly what Uncle George had done with the motorcycle.

CHAPTER TWENTY-ONE

When Scotland Yard is on a man's trail the distinction between night and day is forgot. At half past three in the morning Inspector Bull's telephone jangled insistently. Bull jumped out of bed, cracked his shin on the chair that he had propped against the door to keep the wind from banging it shut, swore vehemently, and barged, wide awake, into the study.

"Hello! Bull speaking. What—*Gates?* Voorhees picked him up? Good Lord! I'll be down in half an hour."

In five minutes Bull had discarded his lavender pajamas, donned his brown Harris tweeds and set out into the biting March night, completely disregarding, in the hurry of the moment, the small grey figure in long outing flannel night shirt, standing wistfully at the head of the stairs. Mr. Pinkerton had waked up too late to join in the hunt.

But Pinkerton had heard enough. He knew much more about the inner organisation of Scotland Yard than anyone

—even Inspector Bull—had any idea of. He spent hours of his solitary little life reading the Police Commissioner's reports and all records that were made public. Sometimes Bull dropped a bit of information without knowing it, and that Pinkerton gathered up and stored carefully away. He knew by name if nothing else almost the entire personnel of the C.I.D.—at least the part of it that was not secret, and even some of the secret members as well. In the present instance, it was enough that Pinkerton heard Bull pronounce the name 'Voorhees'; for he knew that Voorhees was Inspector of the River Constabulary. And when he heard Bull say "Voorhees picked him up!" Mr. Pinkerton knew at once that someone connected with the Colnbrook Outrage had been found in the river.

Mr. Pinkerton decided to start out on his own, and to start at once.

Inspector Bull joined Inspector Voorhees at the mortuary.

"Found him at 3.15," Voorhees explained. "He couldn't have been in long. We'd just gone down, not twenty minutes before—had a call from Woolwich. Started back right away, going pretty fast too. One of the boys spotted him just under Blackfriars Bridge, downstream side. Your man?"

Bull raised the sheet that covered the drowned man.

"I don't know," he said. "Never seen him. Looks like it might be. Eleven stone, thin grey hair, brown eyes, medium height. Look at his hands. They've never done much work. Could be him, easy. I'll get Steiner down to identify him. Monty been in yet?"

Voorhees shook his head. "Telephoned him. Says he'll be down as soon as he can."

"Then I'll get hold of Steiner. Let's see; it's 4.10 now."

"He'll tell you to go to hell, Bull. I would."

"No. He ought to be interested."

Bull groaned as he tried to get his number.

"The girls are bad enough sometimes," he complained, "but the men they get at night are terrible. If I had all the time I've wasted . . . Hello! I want to speak to Mr. Steiner. This is Inspector Bull of Scotland Yard. It's very important. What? He's gone? Well, where *is* he? You don't know? Well, was he there for dinner? All right, was he there at nine o'clock? Well, why the . . . why didn't you say so?"

Bull put down the receiver with a grunt.

"I'm damned," he said simply.

"Try this," said Voorhees. He handed Bull a cup of steaming coffee and a sausage roll. "What's the matter with Steiner?"

"Went to France on the midnight boat from Southampton. No word about when he was coming back."

Bull thought a minute, while Voorhees looked at him with a grin. He picked up the receiver and called Scotland Yard. "Get off a wireless to Southampton, please. I want to know if Albert Steiner, Hatton-garden, is on the midnight boat to Le Havre. Report in half an hour. Get a move on, will you?"

"What are you going to do?" asked Voorhees. "Arrest a decent Jewish merchant because you had to get up at 3.30?"

Bull put down his coffee cup and brushed the crumbs from his coat front. "Go to blazes," he said cheerfully. "I'm not going to arrest him. I want to know where he is. Didn't this man have anything in his pockets?"

"Not a thing. No hat that we could find. We did find something that'll interest you, though. Hey, where's that black satchel?"

Bull groaned inwardly as he took the water-soaked heap that the attendant handed him. He put it on the table and unwrapped it. It was the black satchel, and it was empty. Steiner or no Steiner, there was no doubt left in Bull's mind that the lifeless creature in the next room was James Gates.

He pointed to the small gold initials that were almost illegible with age and use and made more so by their recent soaking. "G. B. C." George Bartholomew Colton.

"This is the satchel that had the diamonds in it," he said. "I think Gates got it when he held them up that night."

"Wonder what happened, Bull? Did he get the wind up and jump in?"

Bull shook his head.

"Why take this with him?"

A young, efficient and very busy police surgeon came in.

"Hello! What's up?"

They went in with him to where the motionless figure lay.

"Picked him up this morning by Blackfriars," said Voorhees. "How long's he been drowned?"

Dr. Montague-Paul looked cheerfully at the figure.

"Your man, Bull?" he asked. "Dryden said you'd never get him. Jolly old Dryden."

"I don't know if I have, yet," Bull said gloomily. "This is one of them, I guess."

Dr. Montague-Paul dropped some of his callous cheerfulness and bent closer.

"You want to know how long ago this fellow was drowned?" he asked.

"Right."

"Well, that's easy. He wasn't drowned at all."

Voorhees looked at Bull. They both looked at the surgeon.

"Have to have the lungs gone into, of course," he said critically. "But I'll lay you a fiver he was dead before he hit the water."

He made a swift examination.

"Here you are."

He pointed to a faint discoloration at the base of the brain.

"Nothing broken, but that's it. He got a blow just here. That's a heavy blow with a blunt, softish instrument—sandbag. Killed him instantly. Have to have an autopsy, Bull, but that's it. I'm going to bed—so long!"

"Well," said Voorhees. "Your case's getting on, Bull. Another murder. Cheer up—the more they get rid of the easier they are to find."

"So they say," Bull said without enthusiasm. "Look here: get hold of Colton's chauffeur for me, will you? Here's the number. Tell him to get down here as quick as he can. I want to use the other line."

He learned that Scotland Yard had just found out that Mr. Steiner was not on board the midnight boat from Southampton to Le Havre.

"Operator can't get him," Voorhees said.

Bull frowned.

"Then I'll go out and get him myself," he said. "If Ames has let him get away. . . ."

"I'll come along," Voorhees said.

Neither spoke until Bull pulled up in front of the Colton garage in Cadogan-square. Bull looked around. No one was in sight.

"Maybe they're both out somewhere, Bull."

"Maybe," Bull grunted.

Then he saw a surprising sight.

"Good Lord!" he said. "There's Pinkerton! What's he doing here?"

The little grey man was peering around the corner of the garage. His face was white. As he saw Bull he came stumbling forward.

"Upstairs!" he gasped. "Something's happened! Quick!"

Bull ran into the open garage and up the steps. The door was wide open, the light was on. Bull took one look and sprang forward. Peskett was lying on the floor, a blackened bullet wound in his forehead. Beside him on the floor a few inches from his hand lay a revolver, and on the table was a little pile of diamonds set in old-fashioned mountings.

Bull knelt down beside the man.

"Give Monty a ring, will you?" he said to Voorhees.

CHAPTER TWENTY-TWO

Bull motioned the two men to stay where they were in the doorway. He got up and moved back to get a wider view of the scene of the third episode of the Colnbrook Outrage.

The chauffeur was lying near the window at the far end of the room. He was in shirt-sleeves and had removed his collar, tie and shoes. A chair was overturned at sharp right angle to the table, as if, Bull thought, he had got up suddenly from examining the jewels spread out there.

Bull said nothing. His mild blue eyes travelled placidly from jewels to table, to chair, to bed, to wardrobe, to each window in turn; and rested at last on the door frame.

"Hmm!" he said then, and looked back at the dead man lying on the floor. Then after a close examination of the floor between the table at which Peskett had been sitting and the open door, he crossed the room and called Scotland Yard.

"Send Bates out. I want some photographs of the place. White to do finger-prints. Be sure to tell the Commissioner as soon as he gets in. I'll be able to be there around noon and I'd like to see him then if he can manage. That's right."

He put down the receiver and turned to Voorhees.

"Will you see if you can find Ames out there anywhere, Ben? Tell him to keep an eye on the house. Nobody is to leave. If he's not there will you stand by?"

Only then did he turn to Mr. Pinkerton. "And what have you been up to?" he demanded.

Mr. Pinkerton had recovered from his agitation, but he did not seem wholly pleased with himself.

"Was that Ames out front?" he asked tentatively.

Bull gave a severe nod. Mr. Pinkerton shifted his feet.

"Well, you see, I heard you say over the phone that you'd be down at once. And I heard you mention Gates and Voorhees. As I knew Voorhees was with the River police I decided they had picked up Gates drowned in the Thames."

"Something of the sort," Bull grunted.

"So I thought there'd ought to be somebody over here to see if Peskett was at home, so I came."

Mr. Pinkerton hurried on without looking at Bull's stony expression.

"I didn't see anybody around but I thought I heard somebody come in the door downstairs. It was dark, but I thought I saw the door move—the shadow, you know. So I crept up and tried it. Just then I heard a noise. I looked around. There was a man creeping up on me behind the hedge. I cut and ran around behind the garage and climbed over the wall. The man was after me. I got into somebody's back garden and had to climb another fence."

Mr. Pinkerton cleared his throat and looked up timidly at Inspector Bull's set face.

"I thought I could go faster than he, but I saw he was gaining on me, so I threw a stone over in the next garden and hid myself behind a holly tree until he'd climbed over that fence. Then I circled back to see what was happening here."

He paused.

"What was?" said Bull, downing his annoyance.

"Well, I'd just got onto the wall when I saw a flash of light. It looked as if it came from a pocket lamp. It was from the Colton's kitchen. I could hardly get over that wall. It wasn't as easy as it was when that man was after me. When I did get over, I thought I heard him in front. I was rather alarmed, because he had blood in his eye when he passed me behind the holly tree. But what I heard in front was you."

Bull took a deep breath and inwardly groaned.

"Yes, it was me," he said simply. "And I suppose you know who the other man was, don't you?"

"I'm afraid it was Mr. Ames," said Pinkerton, with a blush.

"It was," said Inspector Bull. "You've been a great help, Pinkerton."

It was just his luck, he thought, to have such an affair occur while Peskett's murderer got away. For there was not the slightest doubt in Bull's mind that it was murder, although he had not even examined Peskett's revolver to see if it had been fired. It was murder; from the moment Inspector Bull's eyes had rested on the door of the dead man's room he had known it. The bolt that Peskett had put on his door that very morning had been neatly removed.

Ames came up the stairs.

"Nearly got him, sir," he said. "I chased that devil all over the square. But he got away."

He looked at the dead body of the chauffeur and shook his head.

"God!" he said. "I don't see when he did that. I didn't hear a shot. I saw the fellow come out of the door downstairs. He saw me and lit out the back. He was a little fellow but he could run, Inspector! Knows the place too. I'm sorry!"

"All right," said Bull. "Just sets us back is all. Not your fault. You say you didn't hear a shot?"

"No, sir."

"What about earlier? Before that damned man came?"

Ames failed to notice the glance Bull gave his former landlord and closest friend.

"No, I didn't, Inspector."

"All right. See where a bolt has been here? It's gone. Have a look around down in the garage, and in the dust bin, and see if you can find it. Be careful of finger-prints on it if you do. As soon as some of those other people come from the Yard, go along home and get to bed. You look dead to the world."

"Not me. I'm sore as hell, though," Ames muttered. "If I get my hands on that little shrimp I'll break his neck. My shins are raw and I cracked my head on somebody's pergola."

Mr. Pinkerton made an involuntary gesture of dismay.

"You have my permission," said Inspector Bull icily.

Mr. Pinkerton forgot his feelings when he was allowed, for a minute or two, the overwhelming privilege of viewing the Homicide Squad actually at work. They moved in, and moved out again in a quarter of an hour; Mr. Pinkerton, standing timidly in the doorway, could have sworn that nothing in the room had escaped expert attention.

"Have everything ready for you at noon, Bull," said Inspector Bates.

"But you won't get anything off this," said Detective-Sergeant White, motioning to the revolver and wrapping up his finger-printing paraphernalia in an oilskin bag. "Nobody's touched it but him. I can tell you that already. How many shots were fired?"

"One, I guess," Bull said.

"Not out of this," White replied. "Hasn't been fired. Didn't get time, I suppose?"

"He had time enough," Bull said.

Mr. Pinkerton looked eagerly at him.

"That means . . ."

"He was shot by somebody he knew, and by somebody he didn't suspect," said Bull calmly. "And that opens up a lot of fields. Think back to the five possibilities, Pinkerton."

The Homicide Squad departed, Bull stood looking for a minute at the hammer and screw-driver that had been turned up in the bottom drawer of the wardrobe. Then he took the screw-driver over to the door and tried it in the tiny new cuts on the wood trim. They were gouges rather than cuts. Bull put the screw-driver back in the drawer and went over to the day bed in the corner.

"He was lying down," he said to Mr. Pinkerton. "I should say he was ready for something. He had his gun out, anyway. I wonder . . ."

"Hello!" called a cheerful though sleepy voice.

"Right upstairs, Monty," Bull said.

The police surgeon took a quick look around.

"These are busy days, Bull," he said. "Or busy nights, rather. Too damn busy. Suicide?"

"Murder," said Bull.

Montague-Paul knelt down by the chauffeur. He shook his head.

"I can't tell you when this was done," he said, "except that it wasn't a long time ago. Which you already know."

"Was it three hours, or eight hours?" Bull demanded.

"Three or four. That's my guess. The bullet went straight through the right temple. Now wait a minute! This is interesting."

He got up and surveyed the scene.

"He was sitting down here, wasn't he?"

"Looks like it."

"Admiring the pretty baubles here. Well, Bull, he was shot while he was sitting."

Bull looked calmly at him. Mr. Pinkerton eagerly moved up a little, in order to miss nothing. Mr. Pinkerton was just reflecting that this was almost the finest day—or night—of his existence.

"Yes, Inspector," the surgeon went on blandly. "He was shot while he was sitting down—unless by a giant. The bullet was sent down into the lower brain from above. The course, as far as one can tell by a delicate preliminary experiment, diverges noticeably from the horizontal. The bullet enters here, at the lower point of the right temple, and goes down possibly into the cerebellum. That's the part of the brain at the top of your spine."

"So I've heard," said Bull.

Montague-Paul grinned.

"All right. There you are. The assailant was standing about three to two feet away—in other words, close. By the way—I got interested in that fellow Gates, if that's who he is. I didn't go home after all. My diagnosis was right as usual. He was struck a violent blow with a heavy blunt soft instrument at the base of the brain. The brain's clotted and the top of the spine's knocked every which way. He was as dead as Marley when he went into the river. In fact I should say he was deader. Now if you could arrange, Bull, to have no more violence this evening . . . In other words, now I *am* going to retire."

"Just a minute," said Bull. "This man was shot while he was sitting down."

"Or by an eight-footer."

"Why isn't he still sitting down there then?"

The surgeon grinned again.

"Because, my good Bull, he was annoyed. It angered him, it distressed him—in short, he was displeased, he didn't want to be shot in the right temple. So—I'm putting this in the simplest possible way—when shot he arose, he got up, he planned to do something about it."

The surgeon caught Mr. Pinkerton's look of open incredulity and laughed.

"It's quite possible—in fact it's what happened. In getting up he knocked his chair over backwards, to the spot it now occupies. But at that point the motor system failed, naturally. Then the respiratory system failed. Then the heart, some time —not long—afterwards, ceased to function. Just before then he was dead. See?"

"Thanks," said Bull. "I'll try not to call you out again. Tonight, anyway."

They filed down the stairs. At the foot they met Ames.

"Find anything?"

"No luck, sir. Inspector Voorhees said to tell you the people in the house are up, or some of them. In the kitchen, anyway. He said he was getting along. Shall I stay?"

"Get some sleep and come back tonight."

Bull and Mr. Pinkerton continued across the court, passing on their way two men with a stretcher, and went on towards the kitchen. Mrs. Coggins, pale faced and with shaking hands, saw them coming.

CHAPTER TWENTY-THREE

"You're making your rounds early, Inspector," Mrs. Coggins said, stepping aside for Bull to enter.

"You know about the early bird, Mrs. Coggins," Bull replied. He hoped he looked less washed-out than he felt.

"And there's many a truth spoke in jest." Mrs. Coggins looked with some meaning at him.

"That's right, Mrs. Coggins." Then Bull added without changing his tone, "Peskett was shot to death last night."

She stared stupidly at him.

"Peskett?" she said slowly. "Shot to death! Mother of God preserve us!"

She crossed herself hurriedly, then went quickly to the window.

"Is that what those men are busy about out there?" she asked hoarsely. "I thought they'd come because he'd killed the master, God forgive me!"

Bull shook his head.

"He didn't kill your master," he said gently.

"He knew about it," Mrs. Coggins said. She turned quickly away from the window with a shudder, and Bull knew why.

"Only last night at supper it was, Inspector, that he was as cocky as you please, and I said to him, 'Young man, there's many a fool thinks he's a wise man.' "

"What did he say?"

"He said nothing at all. He looked at me queer."

"Who is last to bed in this house, Mrs. Coggins?"

"Usually the mistress."

"Does she lock up?"

"She sees to the front of the house. I do the back."

"Why didn't you lock the kitchen door last night?"

Mrs. Coggins paled.

"I did, sir," she said.

"Who unlocked it, then?"

"Nobody. Not that I know of."

"It was locked when you came down this morning?"

"Yes."

"Think again, Mrs. Coggins," Bull said soberly. "A man's been murdered out there, in cold blood. Shot through the head. Somebody did it. I'm not saying who it was, because I don't know. But I'm going to find out. Now, tell me again. Did you lock the door last night?"

Mrs. Coggins nodded. "Yes, I did," she said.

"But it was not locked this morning—just now—when you came down."

She shook her head weakly.

"How did you know, Inspector?"

"When you let me in just now," Bull explained patiently, "you had to turn the key twice. You locked the door the first time, instead of unlocking it. You had to unlock it then. Do you know who was in the kitchen last night?"

"I don't know."

"Who was in the house?"

"The mistress, Miss Agatha, me, and the parlour maid. Lucy is her name."

"Where are they now?"

"The mistress and Miss Agatha don't get up till nine. That wretched girl should have been down here half an hour ago."

Bull glanced at the little kitchen clock.

"It's eight now," he said. "Wake Mrs. Colton and Miss Agatha Colton and tell them what's happened. Tell them I want to speak to them as soon as possible."

Mrs. Coggins looked intently at him.

"Inspector!" she said. "They didn't have anything to do with it. It's not right, there's nobody to protect them!"

"I only want to talk with them," Bull said patiently. "As soon as possible."

The old woman went out. Bull took the opportunity to make a hasty inspection of the room. He looked in a dozen drawers, and opened the cupboards. When Mrs. Coggins came back he was just where she had left him.

"The mistress will be down in five minutes," she reported. "Poor lamb, it's the first night's sleep she's got in a long time. Sleeping like a baby she was. I had to fair shake her to wake her up. Miss Agatha's coming too. Both of 'em, fast sound asleep.

"The mistress says to go to the library," she added.

She ushered Bull through the pantry, dining room and hall and threw open the library doors.

"Thank you, Mrs. Coggins."

Bull glanced around the room, taking in its details as a matter of habit while he was thinking intently of other things. In a surprisingly short time Mrs. Colton appeared. She was surprising also, Bull thought, in looking much better than when he had seen her last. Her hazel eyes were brighter, her cheeks fuller. And as always, Bull was a little surprised that she wore no jewels of any sort. That she naturally would not be wearing jewels in the morning did not occur to Bull.

She came forward quickly.

"Mrs. Coggins says that Peskett has been shot," she said almost in a whisper. "Is it true?"

"Yes," Bull said.

She closed her eyes. The corners of her mouth trembled. Bull thought she was going to cry.

"It's terrible," she said.

There was a sound in the hall. Bull glanced from the bent, ashen-gold head of Mrs. Colton to her step-daughter. Agatha Colton ignored her stepmother entirely.

"What's this about Peskett?" she said quickly. "Mrs. Coggins says he's dead."

"He was shot this morning, Miss Colton."

Her lithe figure stiffened.

"You don't mean *here?* Not in our garage?"

"Yes. In the room above the garage. He was shot with a revolver, at close range."

Bull looked from one to the other.

"He was going to sail for America next week," Agatha said after a silence. "Poor fellow."

"Did either of you hear a shot?" Bull asked.

They glanced at each other. Each shook her head.

"Agatha's room is on the other side of the house, Inspector Bull. She couldn't possibly."

"And you?"

"No. I heard nothing. I went to bed early, about half past ten. I was very tired. I've not slept much the last two weeks, until last night."

"I slept like a rock," Agatha said abruptly. "I always wake up at six. This morning I slept until I was called. My mouth feels like the bottom of a bird cage."

Bull looked at her in surprise.

"Can't we have a cup of tea here, Louise? I'm most frightfully loggy."

"Surely. Ring, will you please?"

Bull kept to the subject in hand.

"Mrs. Colton," he said clumsily, "do you mind if I search your house?"

She looked at him in amazement.

"What for?" she said blankly.

Bull hesitated. He decided it was better to have it out at once.

"I've no warrant, Mrs. Colton," he said gravely. "But this morning sometime before five o'clock one of my men (how Pinkerton would be pleased, Bull thought) saw a light in your kitchen—a flash from a hand torch. The kitchen door was unlocked when Coggins let me in. If there was someone in your house he might be concealed here now. Because, Mrs. Colton, no one has left—as far as we know. Now as I haven't a search warrant, it's up to you."

Miss Colton intervened sharply.

"I'd get in touch with Field, Louise. You don't know where this may lead."

Mrs. Colton smiled wearily.

"Let's get on with it," she said. "You may search the house, Inspector. Shall I go with you?"

"I'd like both of you to go with me."

Miss Colton laughed.

"There's nobody in my room and here's my tea. I'll drink it first, if you don't mind. Do you mind, furthermore, if I pick up a few of my things before you go in my room?"

"I'd rather not," Bull said placidly. "I shan't disturb anything."

She shrugged her slim shoulders as she poured the tea.

"Louise?"

"Not now. I'll go with Inspector Bull."

In Mrs. Colton's sitting room Inspector Bull glanced out of the open window. He saw his men around the garage, and turned to Mrs. Colton.

"Were your windows open last night?"

"Yes. All of them."

"You didn't hear a shot?"

"Nothing. I slept very soundly."

Bull glanced about the room. He wished he had asked Mrs. Colton to stay downstairs. He was about to ask her to go back to her step-daughter, when, glancing into the mirror of her dressing-table, he caught a glimpse of Mrs. Colton's face. There was an expression of fear in it; and her eyes were riveted on something. She was looking towards the fireplace. Bull looked casually towards it. He could see nothing. The fireplace was perfectly normal. There was a low table by it. On the table was a vase with flowers, and a book.

He glanced away. When he looked at Mrs. Colton she was calmly waiting, her long white hands folded patiently in front of her. Bull had seen something he wanted here; but for appearances he stepped to the wardrobe and opened it. He closed it again.

"That's all here, Mrs. Colton. Miss Colton's room, please."

She led him down the hall to the other side of the house. Agatha Colton's room was a picture of disorder. Filmy garments were flung hastily over chairs; shoes and a hat had been deposited helter-skelter on the chaise longue.

Bull glanced tentatively at Mrs. Colton. She smiled.

"Quite all right," she said. "Agatha never hangs things up. Yesterday was Amy's afternoon off.—I wonder if you'd excuse me a moment?"

"Surely. Why don't you go down and have a cup of tea? I'll only be here a minute—then I'd like to see the other upstairs rooms."

"Thank you!" Mrs. Colton said. "I do need it."

She smiled gratefully at him and went quickly out of the room.

Bull thought a moment, then went quickly to work. He did

102

not have to be very careful. Disorder reigned; he could add nothing to it. He went quickly through the drawers of the dressing table, through the painted boxes of stockings, gloves, lace collars, and cuffs. He looked in her jewel case, which was unlocked and which contained several pieces of jewelry of good quality. He looked in the drawers of the wardrobe, filled with shoes. At last he came to the little make-up table between the windows looking over the garden next door. He opened the lid. In plain sight, dusted with powder, lay the bolt from Oliver Peskett's door; beside it was a small screw-driver, of the kind supplied at Woolworth's. Bull looked at them a minute, then wrapped them together in his handkerchief and put them in his pocket. He closed the top of the poudriére.

He turned just in time to see Miss Colton come in the room.

"Powdering your nose, Inspector?" she asked, smiling with charming impudence.

Bull looked at her gravely.

"Where did you get this, Miss Colton?" he asked. He took the handkerchief from his pocket and unwrapped the bolt and screw-driver.

The smile on her face faded. She looked steadily at them.

"I've never seen them, Inspector Bull," she said quietly.

"They were in your powder table, Miss Colton." He looked at her with mild interest.

"Then you must have put them there," she said. Her black eyes snapped. "What else have you found in my room?"

"Nothing yet. Will you think it over and tell me how this came here?"

The black eyes flashed.

"I can tell you *now*, Inspector Bull, that I don't know. I've never seen either of them before. I'm not a carpenter."

"How did they get here, Miss Colton?"

"I said you probably put them there," she said quickly.

"I assure you I didn't. This bolt, by the way, was taken from Peskett's door last night. It's part of a lock he'd put on it. The person who took it off is probably the person who murdered him."

She looked steadily at him.

"Do you think *I* did it, Inspector Bull?" she asked quietly.

"I don't know who did it, Miss Colton. May I ask you not to say anything about it—not to *anybody?*"

"Of course. Oh, it's too terrible. . . ."

"Thank you. Not *anybody*—do you understand? Not even to Michael Royce."

She smiled suddenly.

"Now one thing more please. Will you see if Mrs. Colton is in her room?"

Agatha Colton looked at him. Then she went quickly down the corridor, tapped gently at Mrs. Colton's door, waited a moment, then opened the door gently. She waved to Bull.

"She must be downstairs."

Bull nodded and went into the room.

He went directly over to the fireplace. The fireplace seemed the same. On the table was the vase filled with flowers, and a book. Inspector Bull grunted happily. The book was red, with a stamped gold title on the spine; but the book that had been there before was red with a printed black title. Bull looked hastily up and down the book shelf at the other side of the fireplace. On a low shelf, half concealed by a chintz-covered chair arm, he spotted the book. He took it out. Inside was a cheque, from Martha Royce to Louise Colton, for £500.

CHAPTER TWENTY-FOUR

Bull put the cheque back in the book, put the book back on its shelf, and went out. The door to Agatha's room was closed, and no one was in sight. He went downstairs; Mrs. Colton was not in the library. Bull was glad. He didn't know exactly what he could say to her. He had other things to do first. He slipped out of the side door and joined Pinkerton and a constable in the garage.

"There's nothing to do here," he said. "You stand by. Better stay inside—and don't let anybody in. After I go you can tell Mrs. Colton that I was called away and I'll see her later. Come along, Pinkerton."

They pulled up outside Victoria Station and went in for a bite of breakfast.

"You'd better get along home now, Pinkerton, and get some sleep," Bull said. The little Welshman was blinking over his porridge like a weary child. "Take the Underground. I'll be out later."

"Can't I go with you?"

"You'll be more help in bed," Bull said with great mildness. Just then he caught sight of himself in the nickel surface of the tea urn. He paid the bill hurriedly.

"See you later," he said. "I'm going to have a wash and get on."

In New Scotland Yard twenty minutes later Bull looked over the reports that had come in.

At 10.43 o'clock on the night of the Colnbrook Outrage a trunk call had been put through from London to the Doaks household in Slough for Field's valet. Doaks had already left for town. The source of the call was impossible to trace; it had been made from a public telephone.

That night also, Doaks had stopped in at the Jolly Farmers at nine o'clock and had stayed ten minutes. He had taken the 10.04 from Slough to London, arriving, as he said, in Mr. Field's chambers in Gray's Inn at half past eleven.

Bull thought about it. It was conceivable that Doaks could have made the distance from Slough to Colnbrook between 9.10, when he left the Jolly Farmers, and 9.25, when Colton was robbed and murdered. Assuming particularly that the clock in the Jolly Farmers was set ahead a minute or so to facilitate ten o'clock closing. Mrs. Colton and the chauffeur had been fairly certain of 9.25 as the time of the murder. Bull chewed the right end of his fine tawny moustache. He then went through the papers in front of him to see what Doaks had been doing the night before.

His shadower had followed him to the market in Lamb's Conduit-street and had observed him doing Mr. Field's marketing for the day. He seemed uneasy, and kept looking behind him furtively. Once he started very definitely, and dropped his greens when he happened to glance at a man standing beside him at the green grocer's. The man was of medium height and build, clean shaven, dressed in a grey lounge suit. Doaks had evidently been mistaken. The man moved away without speaking to him; Doaks showed signs of great embarrassment and tried to explain his actions to the green grocer. The green grocer clapped him on the shoulder, laughed, and gave him some other greens.

Doaks had then returned to the Gray's Inn rooms and gone inside. He came out about nine o'clock and went to a public house—the Clarendon Arms—in Theobald's-road. He sat alone in a corner until closing time. He kept looking up when anyone came in the door, but no one spoke to him, nor did he make or receive any signs. The watcher volunteered the impression that Doaks did not expect anyone but seemed afraid that someone might come.

He had then gone back to Gray's Inn, walking around Red Lion-square to Holborn. At half past ten the lights in the house were turned out. The shadower had waited for two hours. At half past twelve he went to the coffee stall at the foot of Gray's Inn-road and had a snack. He returned ten minutes later and saw a light on the first floor. He watched it until 4.15. He then went back to the coffee stall and had a cup of tea. He was back within ten minutes again. He had just taken his post when the light went out. He then waited until Doaks came down to get the morning papers and milk at 7.30.

Bull allowed himself a sardonic smile and an impatient gesture. Either the fates were against the C.I.D. or, as he was inclined to believe, Doaks was cleverer than Bull had thought.

He reached for the telephone and told the desk man to call off Doaks's shadower. It seemed fairly obvious that Doaks had known he was being watched and had waited until the shadower had gone for a moment. He then slipped out leaving the light burning, and had slipped back during the shadower's second absence.

As for the man in grey at the green grocer's, it was either Peskett, and Doaks gave him a warning that they were observed, or it was not Peskett but Doaks had thought for an instant that it was. If Peskett, it probably explained the evening in the Clarendon Arms—Doaks could have figured that Peskett would look him up. And that brought up again the matter of the connection of the two. Was Doaks afraid of him? His action at the green grocer's seemed to indicate it. Had he got to the end of the rope, gone out to the garage that night and shot Peskett?

Bull shook his head.

That left unexplained the bolt and screw-driver in Agatha Colton's powder table; the flash of light in the kitchen that Mr. Pinkerton had seen; the £500 cheque that Mrs. Colton had tried to hide from him.

Did it explain Gates, who was killed between twelve and half-past three? Bull turned his mind with an effort to the business of Gates; and suddenly remembered that he had said he would be at Albert Steiner's place in Queen's-gate at eight o'clock. Doaks, however, was more important. Bull got his hat. The telephone rang. Bull took off his hat and sat down.

It was Detective-Sergeant Miller, who had been detailed to watch Michael Royce at Windsor.

"What time did he leave? What?"

Bull listened intently. Michael Royce had come out of the Windsor High-street house suddenly, in agitation, had got out the racing Hispano and had come into London, or in the direction of London, at top speed. He had got up to eighty-three miles an hour. Miller, following on a motorcycle, was arrested for speeding at the outskirts of Hounslow. Royce had got away while he was explaining to an angry constable.

Bull sighed and put his hat back on his red-brown head. The telephone rang.

"All right. Tell him I'll be right along."

He took his hat off and hung it up, and went down to see Commissioner Debenham.

"What luck, Bull? Here. You need a peg of this."

The Commissioner got a bottle of Scotch out of his closet and poured Inspector Bull a large glass.

"It's before hours, but we'll take a chance. Now let's have it. What's happened to your four theories, or was it five?"

"They're pretty rocky," Bull admitted ruefully. "I'd better tell you about last night first."

When he had heard Bull's short and matter-of-fact story the Commissioner shook his head.

"Bad, Bull. You'll have to put a stop to this. If we have to have every man in the Yard out. What have you done?"

"Nothing, sir. I've just got to wait."

He told Debenham about the latest development, Michael Royce's wild dash into town.

"This morning Miller went around to Jermyn-street, and there was the Hispano standing in front of Royce's flat. The door man said it was there when he came at seven. The constable on the corner said it had been there since midnight. He knew it was Royce's car."

"So he probably came in from Windsor and went straight there, to Jermyn-street."

"I'll go see, sir," said Bull wearily. "I've also got to see what's happened to Steiner."

Debenham looked up sharply.

"Yes, he's gone too. Then there's the bolt."

The Commissioner smiled a little.

"Bull, you're getting incoherent. What bolt?"

Bull explained.

"When I went out there to find out about the bank deposits, I saw that he had just put a heavy bolt on his door. He didn't care, you see, who came in when he was away. He'd left the door open even. But he didn't want anybody to come in while he was there."

"It seems he had the right idea, Bull." There was a sardonic light in the Commissioner's lean bronzed face.

"Yes."

Bull hesitated.

"Well?"

"Well, sir, he knew somebody had taken the bolt off, I suppose. And he was dressed—mostly, anyway—and he had his gun out. He was ready for somebody. And that's what's queer about it, sir."

The Commissioner nodded his comprehension.

"The person that came wasn't the one he expected."

Bull looked at the Commissioner, who nodded again.

"I see. That brings up something else, doesn't it?"

"And one thing more, sir. It was the first time Mrs. Colton had slept for two weeks; I mean slept well. And Miss Agatha Colton slept very soundly, and complained that her mouth felt like a bird's cage, I think she said."

Debenham frowned. His own daughter used uncouth expressions too. He deplored the modern young woman.

"Well, it's plain that somebody gave them all a mild drug, or a heavy sedative, sir. That's why neither of them heard the shot. It was a small calibre revolver, too."

The Commissioner thought a moment.

"Who was in the house that evening, Bull? I mean, did they have guests?"

"At dinner? I'll see."

Bull reached for the telephone. "Mrs. Royce and Michael Royce were there at dinner. I'll see if there was anyone else."

"Hello! Mrs. Colton? Inspector Bull speaking. What guests did you have in the house last night, please? Thank you."

He turned back to Debenham with a frown on his forehead.

"Well?"

"She says Field and the Royces were there for dinner, and Steiner dropped in for coffee afterwards."

The Commissioner smiled with genuine enjoyment.

"That's a big help, Bull," he observed.

CHAPTER TWENTY-FIVE

"Then there are these, sir," Bull said. He took a little chamois bag out of his pocket. "They're a few of the Royce diamonds. They were on Peskett's table. There's nothing very valuable here; wouldn't come to £50."

"It's a plant?"

"It's a plant, sir. We're supposed to think he's put the rest of them away somewhere."

Debenham took the little assortment of old-fashioned diamond-set trinkets in his hand. He shook his head.

"There's more to it than that, Bull," he said slowly. "I don't understand this."

Bull looked curiously at him.

"Don't you think, sir, that we're dealing with somebody who knows jewels? That stuff's trash compared with stones that used to be worth £35,000."

The Commissioner shook his head again.

"I know what you mean, Bull. But I don't think so. I don't like the idea of these things being left on the man's table. Whoever has done this knows that we wouldn't be fooled by the plant idea. This is tricky, Bull. This looks to me more like a bit of plain bravado; a studied insult to us."

He looked up seriously at Bull's placid face.

"Maybe you're right, sir. Well, if you'll excuse me, I've got to get on with it. There's a lot to do right away."

The Commissioner handed him back the diamonds.

"Right you are. Think about those things, Bull. I have the impression that there was no real purpose in leaving them there, except as a gesture of contempt. Now who would have done such a thing, Bull? Your friend Doaks, for instance? Well, good luck to you."

He smiled as the big young man closed the door behind him.

"You don't know what a pleasure it is," he told Lord Barnham at the Junior Carlton Club at lunch, "to have a man who doesn't pretend to be brilliant, who plods along and then brings off a grand coup as if it had just happened in the natural course of things. He's the only man I've got who hasn't a pet theory. Oliphant with his Reds every time a window is broken in Bond-street, Painter and his chemico-biologico-mechanico-Master-Mind, Dryden and his American racketeers, and the rest of them. Well, Bull's not one of the Big Five yet, but he's going to be in a few years."

Quite unconscious that the Commissioner found him amusing, Bull went back to his room to get his hat and overcoat. A young man was waiting for him; in his hand he had an old grey felt hat.

"Hello, Richards. What's that?"

"Turned in by P. C. 876, sir."

Bull took the hat and looked inside the rim.

"Good man!" he said. "Where'd he get it?"

"On the top of those steps that go down into the water at Trig-lane. Just below Upper Thames-street."

"It was Gates's, all right. 'J. B. G.' Trig-lane; that's near Blackfriars-bridge?"

"Yes, sir."

"Good. This ought to help."

"And there's a telegram. Came up while I was waiting."

Bull picked it up and tore off the envelope. It was from Brussels, and had been received at 10.20 that morning.

"Think it unwise," Bull read, "to stay in London. Please advise Hôtel Angleterre when jewels turn up."

It was signed "Albert Steiner."

Bull read it twice, folded it up without a word and put it in his pocket book.

Downstairs the desk man signalled to him as he was going out. "Call for you, Inspector."

Bull took the telephone and listened to his message without a word. When he had hung up he said to the desk man, "They've found the motorcycle of the Colnbrook affair, or *a* motorcycle, in a woman's garage in Cranford. She's been away two months. It hasn't any licence plates and the serial number's been marked out. When they get it here ask Myers to see if he can identify it."

He went out and hailed a taxi on the Embankment.

"Trig-lane," he said. "Off Upper Thames-street. I'm in a hurry."

Inspector Bull walked down Upper Thames-street. The air was filled with the strong smell of fish. Bull passed St. Andrew's, no longer in use now that no one lived along the river. He turned into the narrow alley known as Trig-lane, and walked down it. At the other end was a constable who saluted him.

"Good morning," Bull said. "You found the hat?"

"Right here it was, sir."

P. C. 876 indicated the spot. Bull looked curiously about him. On either side of the narrow lane the walls of buildings rose sheer; at the river end a flight of steps the width of the lane went down into the water.

Bull looked at them.

"A man who didn't know where he was could get a surprise going down those steps," he remarked.

"He could, sir, and that's a fact."

"The hat was here?"

"Yes, sir. It was all crumpled up, like somebody had stepped on it."

Bull nodded.

"How did you happen to come down here?"

"Well, you always come down here, sir. It's a bad place. I always said something ought to be done about it. There's not a soul about these parts at night, sir, and no lights at all. I always say it's a wonder more people don't go down them steps."

Bull agreed.

"Who'd you relieve last night?"

"Porter, sir. I asked when I come on if he'd heard anything. There was talk at the station about picking up a man under the bridge. But he hadn't. A parcel of the fishmongers got in a fight down the street, and he had his hands full down there."

"The hat was crumpled?"

"That's right, sir. Mind you don't go over."

Bull got up from his knees. There was probably not much question about what had happened. There were new scratches on the top step. Bull thought it was not hard to figure out.

He found a telephone in a warehouse in Upper Thames-street and after some trouble heard the sleepy voice of P. C. Porter. Porter lived in the basement of a house in Robin Hood-court; in ten minutes he was dressed and waiting for Inspector Bull at the door of St. Andrew's.

"Sorry to get you out," Bull said. "But a man was murdered last night at the bottom of Trig-lane. You didn't report any disturbance?"

"Disturbance enough on Thames-street, there was, sir. They were crazy drunk, the lot of them. I'd of turned in a riot call if they'd been one more."

"What time was that?"

"That was at eleven, sir. Three of 'em got in an argument with some of the barge men about a rat—who's rat it was, that was what they was fighting about. They'd all had more'n a drop. It was rightfully the barge people's rat, to my mind, if they wanted it. But no. There was that rat."

Constable Porter pointed graphically to an imaginary rat on St. Andrew's porch, and Bull listened patiently, knowing that constables must tell their story in their own way.

"And there was the fishmongers. One of them had a stick and was for thrashing the rat. The bargemen says, 'That's our rat.' One of them gets a pole. His pole was bigger than the fishmonger's stick. Then one of the bargemen says the others was spoiling their rat, he'd stink of fish. Well, then the rat went down there. Then they was all sore and they started to fight."

"What did you do?"

"I let 'em fight until a few of 'em was hurt bad enough

so I could manage the rest," said Porter. "Then I took all of 'em up for disturbing the peace."

"That was around eleven."

"Yes, sir."

"Where were you between twelve and three?"

"Walking up and down. Clemson and me go from the bridge to Cannon-street. But he was off, because he took sick of a sudden and I sent him back to the station. Nothing ever happens along here except like last night, but that's all in fun. The only other people ever down here are regulars. Are you sure that person wasn't done in somewheres else?"

Bull shook his head.

"He was murdered with a heavy blow on the head, and it was done at the bottom of the lane."

Constable Porter looked his lack of understanding.

"I don't see how it happened, sir."

"You said nobody but regulars were down here. What do you mean?"

"Why, there's an old woman that sleeps here, in the doorway over yonder. She hangs about the fishmongers. Lizzie, they call her. Harmless, she is. She gets a bunch of violets and carries 'em about in the daytime. Then there's Joe. He sleeps at the bottom of Broken-wharf. Maggie sleeps in a door-step across from the fish-and-chips shop in Dean-street out of Robin Hood-court where I live. She's around here a good bit in the evening with Lizzie. People give 'em mussels and oysters and a bit of fish now and again."

Bull nodded.

"Where could I find Lizzie, do you think?"

"Couldn't say, sir—not till night-time. She'll be here then sure as you're born."

"All right, Constable," Bull said. "I'll be here at midnight. Keep an eye on Trig-lane for me, will you?"

Bull went back to Blackfriars and up to Fleet-street.

"Hello, Bull," he heard as he passed the entrance to the *Evening Telescope*. It was Walters.

"I met Debenham, Bull, and he said you've got Gates."

"Yes," Bull said. "Got him dead."

"Too bad. What about a story?"

"Come with me tonight and you might get one. I'm checking up on the Gates business. But it's got to be quiet for a while."

"Right you are. What about a spot of dinner?"

Bull grinned.

"Make it about eleven? I've got a full day."

"All right. Make it eleven, at the Ship. Cheerio."

Bull started to take a taxi and changed his mind. He went along Fleet-street to Chancery-lane, up to Holborn, across and up the little lane into Jockey's-fields and rang the bell on Mr. Field's front door.

CHAPTER TWENTY-SIX

The appearance of another motorcycle had relieved the tension about Doaks to some extent; but Bull thought that he had still left a good deal to explain, and it was impossible for Bull to leave a trail until he was perfectly convinced he had come to the end of it. And he was now fully aware that he had the vaguely uneasy feeling that the two murders, of Peskett and Gates, were not necessarily done by the same hand that had shot down the St. Giles-street jeweller in cold blood.

The feeling had been struggling in his subconscious mind since the moment he saw the dead body of the chauffeur lying in front of the window in the upper room of the garage. It was different in some way. What Debenham had said was true. The murder of Peskett was not done with as fine free a hand as marked the death of Colton, nor yet with the subtle desperation of the blow struck in Trig-lane.

The more Bull thought of it the more convinced he became that he was right. The thing was gradually taking form, rounding itself out before him. And it may be said in Bull's favor that he was not very happy about it. In fact he was distinctly horrified.

The man—and he was convinced that there was a man— who chose the spot on the Colnbrook Road to hold up and shoot George Colton—was the man who chose the bottom of Trig-lane to strike the blow that felled Gates. The handwriting—as it were—of the two was the same. Calm, brutal, ruthless, decided. So was the murder of Peskett. Here was the difference: whoever had done the first two had not tried to involve anyone else. They were not crafty, except in their perfect simplicity; they were not devilish. The murder of Oliver Peskett was carefully planned, and the planning included the laying of false trails, the implication of other people. That murder was as devious as the others were simple. The two were unscrupulous but keen and level-headed; the one was scheming, cruel, vindictive. And the jewels on Peskett's table. Bull pondered over the Commissioner's words. Was that a sardonic contemptuous gesture? It was in keeping.

Bull knew—or thought he knew—that a man had done

113

two of these crimes, a woman the other. They were as clearly finger-printed as if an ungloved hand dipped in blood had gripped the ivory painted edge of Agatha Colton's powder table.

All this had gone through his head between the time he rang the doorbell and Doaks's opening the door. Bull did not miss the glint of sickening fear that flashed across his pasty face.

"I want to see Mr. Field," Bull said.

"Yes, sir. He's been trying to call you on the phone all morning."

Bull followed upstairs. He was shown into a long room overlooking the gardens of Gray's Inn. He sat down in a deep lounge chair by the fire. It was the sort of a room that he always thought of when he heard the word "chambers," although he knew very well that few chambers were like it. Three walls were book-lined in mellow calf with tooled backs. Here and there a bright modern red or chrome yellow accented the soft browns of the past. A few French and German paper books bobbed up indiscreetly here and there. A deep pile Oriental carpet and Jacobean furniture added to the quiet restful dignity of the room. Bull forgot he was in a Georgian house. It was as old and restful as eternity to him just then. The wintry sun filtered through long, deep, russet velvet hangings at the windows. Bull closed his eyes. He suddenly realized that he was dog-tired and starving—and as nervous as a cat, he realised, when Mr. Field's voice behind him startled him.

"Good morning, Inspector. I'm glad you've come. Sit down. Agatha Colton telephoned me about Peskett."

"Yes?" Bull said. "It's a bad business. I want to talk to you about that, and about the whole affair, as a matter of fact."

"Good. Look here, you look dog-tired. Let me get you a whiskey and soda, or would you rather have some coffee and biscuits?"

"Thanks. I'll have the coffee."

Field stepped out of the room. He returned in a moment and sat down on the other side of the hearth.

"I'm not sure what the coffee will be like," he said with a smile. "Doaks looks as if he'd seen his mother's ghost."

"He's one of the things I want to talk about," Bull said, leaning forward. "What do you know about him?"

Field looked at him in mild surprise.

"About Doaks?" he asked. When Bull nodded he laughed quietly.

"What does it matter, Inspector?" he said. "Poor fellow!"

114

Bull for a moment thought Field was speaking of him.

"Doaks was in the war—gathered off the streets of London like thousands of other men, thrown into a life that was hard enough for the best, and then thrown out again, dazed, bewildered, nothing to do, nowhere to go. Their holes had been filled up with more just like them. They gradually got to crawling again. Doaks was typical. His father lived in Slough, his wife died and he married again, a London costermonger's daughter. She couldn't stick it and ran away, back to her father's barrow. Brought her baby along with her. Doaks learned to cook somewhere, and I ran across him in the dock at Old Bailey. I got him off. He's been with me three years. He's no better and no worse than he has to be. I watch him carefully."

"Ever had any trouble with him, Mr. Field?"

"None. He steals my wine and spirits at times. You expect a certain amount of that. He has careless streaks. He's shiftless at times." Mr. Field grinned deprecatingly. "So am I, at times. Doaks has more reason on his side."

Bull was becoming aware that he liked Field.

"Look here," he said, "what about last night. When did Doaks get in?"

"Soon after ten. I was reading in here. He came in to see if I wanted anything. I was tired; I've been holding a very exacting brief. He brought me some biscuits and went to bed. I turned in about 11.30. He brought my tea at 8.00 this morning."

Doaks came into the room carrying a silver coffee service and set it down on the low table at Inspector Bull's elbow. He poured a cup of fragrant coffee.

"Cream, sir?"

Bull nodded.

"Sugar, sir?"

"Two."

"That's all, thanks, Doaks."

The valet went out of the room and closed the door noiselessly behind him.

Bull sipped his coffee gratefully for a moment. Then he set his cup down on the heavy carpet. Noiselessly he rose and went to the door. Field, looking on in amazement, could not believe that he saw the enormous man move so swiftly and silently. It was incredible. He looked at Bull with increasing interest. Up to now he had regarded him as a clumsy, stolid, amiable person who had some reputation for reasons unknown. He wondered now if there were not some persons underestimating Bull.

Bull opened the door suddenly. Mr. Doaks was busily cleaning the woodwork across the narrow hall. He turned with a palpable start.

"Something, sir?" he said.

"Nothing," Bull replied. "You're through there, aren't you?"

"Yes, sir."

Bull closed the door and came back to his place. Field watched him with a quiet smile.

"You didn't hear him go out during the night?"

"No, I didn't, Inspector. Oh, there was one thing. I woke up about half past four and saw a light under the door of my room. It was in the dining room."

"Didn't you leave it on when you went to bed?"

"No. I went to my room from here, I wasn't in the dining room. Doaks probably left it on when *he* went to bed. He frequently does. He's careless about a good many things. So I never attach any importance to it. When I see a light left on I get up and turn it off. I happened not to notice it when I went to bed or I'd have done it then."

Bull thought a moment. Then he said, "What would you say, Mr. Field, if I told you that that light didn't go on until after half past twelve?"

"I'd say you were crazy," replied the solicitor, with a disarming smile.

Bull shook his head.

"I'm not," he said. "One of my men was watching your house for Doaks last night. He reported that light. He knows when it went on, and when it went off."

John Field looked at him steadily. It was a relief to Bull to find a man who didn't jump and look horrified at the least provocation.

"Let me get Doaks in here and ask him about it," Field said at last. "It won't be the first time I've examined him."

Bull nodded, and Field reached for the bell pull.

Doaks came in. Bull noticed that his face was ashy. Field motioned him to a place between them.

"Bring up that chair, Doaks, and sit down. Look here. Where were you last night?"

"Here, sir," Doaks's agitation increased rapidly.

"Pull yourself together," Field said quietly. "If you're in a jam you know you can count on me—don't you?"

"Yes, sir."

"Then let's have it. Where were you last night?"

"I was here, sir, and that's God's truth, so help me. I went out to the public in Theobald's-road and at closing time I walked around Red Lion-square into Holborn and home, sir. I brought you some biscuits and then I went to bed. I wasn't out of the house."

Field looked at him a second without speaking. Then he said, "What did you go in the dining room for?"

Doaks looked at him in despair.

"Did I leave that light on, sir?"

"You did."

"I'll take the sack, sir. But I was fair potty, what with this fellow Peskett and the police, never knowing which way to turn. You'd said it was the sack for me next time I did it, but I couldn't help it, sir."

Bull glanced at Field and Field at Bull.

"Out with it," Field said sharply but not unkindly.

"I got drunk, sir. I don't know rightly what I did, except I finished off what was left in the decanter. I went to bed. Then I heard you go in your room and I came down and got a glass and helped myself."

"What did you do then?"

"I went to bed, sir."

Field glanced at Bull, who nodded.

"All right, Doaks. We'll talk about it later."

"That's probably the truth," he said to Bull when the door had closed behind the servant. "He can't keep away from it at times."

They sat in silence a few moments while Bull assorted what he'd heard with what he knew already and what he suspected, and laid it carefully away for future use.

"Another thing," he said after a bit. "You said Mrs. Colton was a wealthy woman, didn't you?"

Field nodded and looked inquiringly at him.

"Is it ready money, or is it tied up?"

"It's tied up as well as legal and financial ingenuity can devise—for a while," Field said after a moment's thought. "You see," he added with a frank smile, "I hesitate to tell you Mrs. Colton's business unless in her presence."

"You needn't," Bull said soberly. "I can find it out elsewhere. It's simpler this way. Otherwise I have to serve papers and all that."

"I suppose you're right. You see Mr. Colton was afraid his wife would marry at once when he died. He had somebody in mind too, a doctor fellow I think. He was a very jealous man, Inspector. To protect her—or so he used to put it—he tied his funds up in hard knots; so hard, in fact, that he was pretty much strapped himself at times. But that's neither here nor there. His daughter's money he left fluid. She has £1000 a

117

year that's paid regularly under the will. Mrs. Colton has no ready cash, not for six months, I think. I did my best to get him to change it, but he wasn't having any pill dispenser and bone setter taking a holiday at his expense as soon as he was underground."

Bull said nothing for a moment. What was the name of that doctor who was brought in for Smith? The man's face came back with a rush into his memory. Could it be possible . . . ? Bellamy, that was it.

He came back into the present and found Field looking curiously at him.

"Can you tell me who Mrs. Colton would be most likely to go to if she needed money?" he asked.

"Me," said Field. "I could always advance her anything she needed, or arrange it for her through her bank."

"Has she come to you?"

"No. She drew quite a bit from Colton a week or so before his death, I think, and she had something in her banking account."

"If she needed cash would she be apt to go to—say—Mrs. Royce?"

Field looked at him and broke into a hearty laugh.

"About as much as a canary would go to a vulture," he said without hesitation.

Inspector Bull gathered that Field was not fond of the dragon who lived in Windsor.

CHAPTER TWENTY-SEVEN

After Bull left John Field he made his way across Holborn and down Chancery-lane to the Kardomah Coffee Shop. He hardly realised that it was after three o'clock until he settled himself, ordered a light lunch, and picked up an afternoon edition of the *Standard*. He glanced through it and picked up a morning paper that was on the bench. His eye struck a column that annoyed him more than he had been annoyed for months.

"The most vigorous and sustained man hunt ever to take place in the Metropolitan police area," it said, "has gone on since the brutal robbery and murder of Mr. George Colton, St. Giles-street (Bond-street) jeweller, on the Colnbrook Road at 9.25 o'clock Wednesday evening, February 25th.

"Last night Mr. Colton's chauffeur, Oliver Peskett, was shot to death in his room above the garage of the Colton home in Cadogan-square.

"So far the perpetrator of these two appalling tragedies is at liberty in spite of the efforts of the police.

"It is useless to disguise the fact that unless the unforeseen happens he is likely to evade the police. Regrettable and alarming as this may be, it has to be recognised that it is no fault of the Scotland Yard officers, who have been, and of course, still are, pursuing their investigations.

"The Murder Squad is working under the able supervision of Chief Inspector Luther Dryden and Detective-Inspector J. H. Bull."

Inspector Bull put the paper down with a scowl and hurriedly finished his lunch. Then he rubbed his stubbly chin and decided he'd better get a shave before he went any further.

Three quarters of an hour later he presented himself at Michael Royce's flat in Jermyn-street, and was glad he was not five minutes later.

A taxi stood in front of the building. The burly driver was tying a steamer trunk marked M.C.R. onto the top. Two large leather portmanteaux, a bristling golf bag, and a tan rain coat were piled on the pavement. Bull rang the lift bell and listened intently at the grated cage. He heard it coming, stepped outside again and took another look at the taxi and its driver. He returned and stepped into the lift.

"Mr. Royce, please."

"Mr. Royce is going away. I don't think he's seeing anybody, sir."

"Mr. Royce," said Bull, "and make it quick."

On the third floor Michael Royce was writing a note at a secretary in the corner of the sitting room. He turned sharply when Inspector Bull opened the door and walked in.

"What do you mean by this?" he said angrily.

Bull was pleased.

"A chip of the old block for all his manner," he thought.

Aloud he said, "I want to find out something about last night, Mr. Royce."

Royce mastered his anger with an effort.

"*What* about it?" he said. "I wish you'd get on with it. I'm due at Croydon at 5.10."

"Going away?" Bull said blandly.

"Right."

"I wish you wouldn't," Bull remarked. "I'd like you to wait a few days."

He saw the rising tide of anger in Royce's face.

"Why do you say that, Inspector?" he said thickly.

"There are a number of reasons, Mr. Royce," Bull said quietly. "The chief is that Oliver Peskett was shot dead last night at Cadogan-square."

Royce stared at him.

"What do you mean? You don't mean the Coltons' driver —*that* Peskett?"

"I do," said Bull. He walked into the room and·sat down. "What are you leaving for, Mr. Royce?"

"I'm leaving . . ."

Royce stopped stubbornly and said nothing. He stared down at the rug. Somewhere a bell buzzed gently. He paid no attention to it.

A patient voice spoke from the hall.

"Shall I tell them you're out again, sir?"

Bull looked around. A tall thin man with an air as tired and patient as his voice stood in the doorway.

Royce got up suddenly.

"No. I'll answer it."

Bull made a move as if to stop him and changed his mind. With mild interest he watched Royce leave the room. He beckoned to the servant.

"I'm Inspector Bull of New Scotland Yard," he said. "Has Mr. Royce not been answering the telephone today?"

"No, sir. He said this morning that he was not in, no matter who called. Not in exactly those words. That was his meaning."

Bull gathered that the words had been more violent.

"Why?"

"He didn't give any reason, sir. He was that upset that I guessed why, though."

"What's wrong?"

The man looked over his shoulder cautiously and lowered his voice.

"It's his young lady, sir. Miss Colton. She's very difficult. She leads him a merry dance, as they say. And as his temper's not as sweet as sugar—perhaps you know his mother, sir?"

Bull nodded. It was easy to understand.

"But it's his mother that's been calling him all day, not Miss Colton. Now usually after they've quarrelled she always telephones the next day and says she's sorry. Then everything's lovely. But she's not called today, sir, not once."

There was distinct concern in the man's voice.

"Where was Mr. Royce last night?"

The servant did not have time to answer. Michael Royce came back into the room. His jaw was set rigidly, but his dark eyes were troubled. Bull read more than worry in them; they contained fear.

"Get my things up again, Jenkins," he said. "I'm not going. Here, give that man this and help him get my box down."

He handed the servant a ten-shilling note and moved over to the fire-place, where he stood moodily, his hands in his pockets, staring absently into the fire.

Bull watched him a moment, and sat down.

"What did you and Miss Colton quarrel about last night?" he asked abruptly.

"We didn't quarrel," Royce returned almost absently. "I suppose Jenkins told you that. Every time I go to France he thinks it's because I've quarrelled with Miss Colton. He happens to be wrong this time."

"You quarrelled with your mother then?"

"Yes. If you're interested, I did."

"What about, please."

"That's our business, Inspector."

"Who were at the Coltons' last night?"

Royce looked at him steadily.

"I was there, Mother, Field. We were there at dinner. After dinner Steiner, the jeweller, came in for coffee."

Bull hesitated a moment. Then he asked, "Who served the coffee?"

Michael looked at him in genuine surprise.

"Why, Mrs. Colton poured it and the maid passed it.—No, she didn't; I did. The maid went out and I made myself useful."

Bull looked at him placidly.

"Who left first, Mr. Royce?"

"Steiner. He said he was leaving for a few weeks for the continent. Business. He wanted to see if he could do anything for Mrs. Colton. They went out into the hall together. She came right back. Then Field left. He was tired. Or he said so, and looked it. Mother and I went about nine, I should say."

"You had your quarrel on the way home?"

Royce said nothing.

"After you left Windsor at 10.45 where did you go?"

Royce looked at him with a start.

"That ass that's been following me about for a week is one of your men, is he?"

121

"That's right."

"Then he can tell you. He hasn't been five steps away from me. I've had to push him aside to get at my meals."

"He lost you outside Hounslow," Bull said. "You were doing eighty-three. He was trying to keep up with you and a constable arrested him for dangerous driving."

Royce smiled slightly. His eyes did not lose the deep troubled look of anxiety or worse.

"In that case," he said, "I'll tell you that I came here and started packing up to go to France."

"Why the hurry?"

"No hurry. I merely wanted to get away as soon as possible. Reasons of my own."

"Those reasons are very important to me, Mr. Royce. Think about what's happened here these last two weeks."

Royce shrugged.

"Did you know . . . Gates?"

Bull watched him closely.

"Colton's clerk? Yes. I knew him when I was a child. I've seen him once or twice since. Why? Has he turned up?"

"Yes, he's turned up. I want you to identify him."

"*Identify* him?"

Royce looked at the Inspector. Bull saw that his hands were shaking.

"You don't mean that he's dead too? My God, this is a perfect shambles! It's horrible!"

"It *is* horrible," Bull said. "Can you go now?"

He saw that Royce was hard hit; he was making a great effort to regain his self-possession.

"Jenkins, I'm going with Inspector Bull. I will go out to Windsor then. I won't be back until late."

"Very good, sir."

This, Bull felt, was a message for Agatha Colton in case she did telephone.

"Shall we take my car? I'll have them send it around."

"Right. If you don't mind I'll run out to Windsor with you when we're through."

They drew up in front of the mortuary and got out. An old woman, toothless and in rags, came out as they went in. Bull heard her speaking to the constable at the door in a whining sing-song voice.

"It ain't my Jawn, 'e's not so young as 'im."

She wiped her watery eyes with her filthy ragged sleeves and sniffled pathetically. They stood aside for her as she hobbled out of the door, and went down the corridor into the room where the body of the man who had been dragged out of the river lay waiting. Bull uncovered the dead face. Royce's hands clenched involuntarily.

"That's Gates," he said.

A little later they were on the way to Windsor. Royce had not spoken since he made his sworn statement at the mortuary. Bull was content to let him take his time. It was he who broke the silence as they slipped swiftly through Cranford.

Bull pointed to a house whose high privet hedge concealed the garden from the road.

"There's where they found the motorcyle yesterday," he said.

"What motorcycle?"

Bull smiled. Royce seemed to know surprisingly little about the Colnbrook case generally, and had less interest.

"The motorcycle used by the man who killed and robbed Mr. Colton."

"Oh. Can you trace it?"

"I don't think so. It might have finger-prints on it somewhere. Very often, you see, the clever criminal overlooks the very simplest thing. He may have wiped off the whole thing and missed one spot, or a piece of his trousers-cuff may have caught in the pedal. You can't ever tell. It's just such things that hang people."

Royce said nothing. They lapsed into another silence that lasted until they drew up in front of Mrs. Royce's house in the High-street.

Mrs. Royce was waiting for them in her sitting room on the first floor. She got up when they came in, leaning on her stick, glowering at them ominously.

"Good morning, Inspector. Michael, come here!"

Michael obeyed. Bull half expected her to pick up the stick and give him a caning on the spot. He held himself ready to interfere if necessary to prevent violence, or too great violence. He was not ready for what actually happened. When her son was within two feet of her, she put out her arms and drew him close to her. He let his head sink a moment on her ample bosom, and she patted his shoulder gently.

"There, my boy," she said softly. Her deep voice was vibrantly tender.

It passed in an instant. Bull was still staring stupidly at them. She pushed Michael roughly away.

"Don't be a fool, boy," she said. "Pick up my stick. I'm glad you've come to your senses—didn't think you would. Now what's all this that's happened?"

"Gates is dead, Mother. I went to identify him. He was drowned."

"He was not drowned, Mrs. Royce," Bull said. "He was struck over the head and thrown in the water."

"Inspector!" cried Mrs. Royce; "where is this going to stop? Gates was coming to see me this morning. He wrote me a letter. In my leather envelope, Michael, downstairs. I can't make much out of it."

She made her son an imperious sign.

"Don't stand there like a half-wit, Michael, go get it."

He left the room. Mrs. Royce sat down heavily.

"Sit down, Inspector Bull," she said. "I'm an old woman. These things are beginning to terrify me. I think I was wrong in stopping Michael from going abroad."

"If you hadn't, ma'am, I should have done so," Bull said bluntly.

She looked at him. Her lips closed tightly. She shrugged her shoulders.

The door opened and Michael Royce came back.

"Give it to me," she said, holding out her hand.

"You must have been mistaken, Mother," her son said evenly. "There was no letter there."

She stared at him dumbly.

"I . . . mistaken?" she gasped slowly. She sank down in her chair. "Perhaps you're right," she said then, faintly.

Inspector Bull stood up.

"Perhaps the letter has been stolen, Mrs. Royce?"

Mrs. Royce was silent. Then she raised herself erect in her chair.

"I must not have saved the letter, Inspector," she said.

CHAPTER TWENTY-EIGHT

Bull looked calmly at the two. There was no evidence of the abruptness of his mental about-face as he rapidly recast several of his ideas.

He went across the room to Royce.

"Let me have the letter, please," he said.

Royce held up his hands promptly. "I haven't got it," he said. "Search me if you want to."

"I don't need to do that," Bill replied. "Will you excuse me, ma'am?"

He bowed and left the room. He closed the door deliberately. In the hall his manner changed; he was at the head of the stairs in two strides and down them in five, silently on the heavily carpeted steps. Quickly and quietly he went down the lower hall and turned the handle of Mrs. Royce's sitting room. A glance into the cold fire-place was enough; a few black cinders were all that was left of the letter that Gates had written to Mrs. Royce. Michael had even scattered them with the poker.

Inspector Bull let himself out the front door into the High-street. Walking slowly up the hill he glanced at the statue of the good queen. A famous remark of hers that precisely fitted his own feelings came into his mind. "We are not amused." Bull had never been less so in his life.

He turned left to the station. On the train he thought how nearly he had come to taking the Royces, both of them, into his confidence. He had come to Windsor for the sole purpose of asking Mrs. Royce why she had given Mrs. Colton the cheque. He had underestimated the old lady. He had failed to realise that her love for her son was greater than her idea of duty to the Crown. That was his mistake, and a stupid one. He should never have permitted it, but he had been so persuaded of the young man's innocence that he had dismissed the vague warning that he felt when Mrs. Royce sent her son after the letter. It had not occurred to him that Royce was desperate. The set-up was changing radically.

Bull looked at his watch. It was close to seven o'clock. He put his feet up on the seat across from him, pulled his hat down over his eyes and slept peacefully until the guard tapped his arm at Paddington. He got a hurried bite to eat and took a taxi to the Embankment. He had many things to do before he went to dine with Walters.

On the desk were various reports from men following diverse tracks to a common meeting place, or so Bull hoped.

1. It had proved impossible to trace the motorcycle. A woman in Cranford—she whom the police thought un-reliable—had seen a car parked behind the hedge about nine o'clock. At half past nine she heard a motorcycle somewhere on the road. There was no doubt now that she had really heard Colton's murderer. The serial number had been carefully and thoroughly obliterated. The cycle could not be identified.

2. A bullet fired at about two feet distance from a .22 calibre revolver had killed Oliver Peskett.

3. A woman operative who had taken the place of the Coltons' house-maid, suddenly taken ill, had found an empty phial of one-half grain phenol barbital tablets in the dust-bin in the kitchen. A few such tablets would insure unusually

sound sleep. They were tasteless, but might leave a furry condition of the mouth the next morning and cause a general sleepiness.

4. The unknown man picked up in the Thames was identified by Michael Royce, Jermyn-street, under oath, as James B. Gates, age unknown, clerk at the jewelry shop of Mr. George Colton in St. Giles-street. The time of his death was approximately two o'clock.

5. The constable on duty in Bond-street had glanced down St. Giles-street at 12.53 A.M. and seen a man apparently trying to get into the padlocked shop of the late George Colton, jeweller. He had given chase but the man eluded him.

Bull stopped and glanced again at the time of that occurrence. 12.53 A.M. Bull smiled happily. The pieces were fitting together; he did not despair of getting his jig-saw puzzle to look like something. The heads of some important figures were forming with unmistakable clarity. He could name four men who were in London last night at 12.53.

6. Albert Steiner had left Croydon by special plane at six A.M. that morning and arrived at Le Bourget an hour and ten minutes later. The manager of the Hôtel Angleterre in Brussels verified the statement that Steiner was staying there.

7. At 6.30 that afternoon Doaks had left the house only to go to market and directly back.

8. Mrs. Louise Colton had deposited a cheque for £500 to her personal account at Coutts's Bank in Piccadilly.

9. Miss Agatha Colton had gone on a shopping trip in Knightsbridge in the afternoon and returned home shortly after five o'clock.

Bull left a note for the commissioner and went out. He hailed a taxi and gave the driver the Coltons' address.

The maid who opened the door looked quickly around her before she stepped aside to let him in.

"Is Mrs. Colton in?"

"Yes, sir. I'll tell her you're here. She's upstairs."

"I'll wait in the library."

The young woman was back in a moment.

"Is Miss Colton in?" Bull asked quietly.

The girl smiled. Bull wondered, as he had done before, how people could possibly think she was actually a parlour-maid. Her intelligent dark eyes, her poise, her tone of voice were anything but those of a servant girl. Bull had never seen the cow-like glaze in her eyes as she explained to a new mistress that a favourite piece of bric-a-brac had just jumped right out of her hands onto the floor.

126

"She's packing. She sulked all morning. Asked me every five minutes if Mr. Royce hadn't called her. They had a lovers' quarrel last night, Mrs. Coggins says. She went out at three and came in about five."

"What for? Do you know?"

The girl smiled again. "I went up to straighten her room—that's the parlour-maid's chief job here, cleaning up after her. She was trying to pack. I think she was just getting things she needed for travelling. She called me just after she came in. She told me to tell Mrs. Colton she was going to Paris."

Bull smiled indulgently. The girl vanished just as Mrs. Colton came into the library.

"Good evening, Inspector Bull," she said. "I've been lying down. Will you sit down?"

She motioned him to the chair across from her and leaned her head wearily against the velvet back of the chair Bull had drawn forward for her.

She did look tired, Bull thought. He realised again that she was a very beautiful woman.

He came at once to the point.

"Mrs. Colton, you put a cheque for £500, given you by Mrs. Royce, in the bank today. I have to ask you why Mrs. Royce gave you that money."

Mrs. Colton flushed and drew her breath sharply.

"I'm afraid I rather resent this prying into my personal affairs, Inspector Bull. I don't mind your searching my house, and I don't particularly mind your putting a person in the house who obviously isn't a parlour-maid. As a matter of fact she's extremely intelligent and has been very useful, though it's annoying never to turn your back without feeling she's going through your writing table or dust-bin. But I do particularly object to your interfering with my banking arrangements."

"I'm sorry," Bull said apologetically. "But you see, Mrs. Colton, your husband was shot. His clerk was killed. Your chauffeur was shot and killed in his room over your garage. It's my job to follow any clue I have, no matter who it annoys. So I have to ask you that question. Why did she give you the money?"

"Because, Inspector Bull," Mrs. Colton said coldly, "I have no money. I needed it, and I asked her for it."

"Why did you go to Mrs. Royce, instead of your bank, or Mr. Field?"

She looked at him with a half-smile on her lovely face.

"Because I preferred to go to Mrs. Royce," she said calmly.

Bull looked placidly at her from his mild blue eyes.

"Mrs. Colton!" he said. "You can't do this. You don't understand your situation."

"On the contrary, Inspector Bull, I understand it entirely."

"I'm afraid you don't."

She seemed astonished at his persistence.

"You knew, of course, that Mrs. Royce's diamonds were insured for £35,000, and that they worth about £10,000 on the market?"

Mrs. Colton was an intelligent woman. He hoped he wouldn't have to go any farther. She sat staring absently into the fire, apparently unaware that he was still in the room. Finally she looked up and smiled frankly.

"I do understand my position," she repeated; "but I'm quite prepared to cope with it. Let me tell you something."

She leaned forward, her elbow on her crossed knee, her chin in her palm. She looked into the fire, not at Bull.

"Mr. Steiner was here the night Peskett was shot.—Was that only last night?"

For an instant the horror of it came back to her, and she closed her eyes.

"It seems centuries ago," she said softly. An involuntary tremor seemed to ripple through her body. Then she drew a deep breath and went on.

"Steiner told me that Mr. Colton had made an arrangement with him that he had accepted with reluctance. He had done so, however—agreed to it—in view of a number of things. One of them—although he didn't mention it—is his almost morbid passion for diamonds. My husband needed ready money. In the last two years he has tied up all of his money up so that in the event of his death I couldn't get my hands on it for some time. As a result, when money suddenly tightened up so decidedly, he found himself in a difficult place. He couldn't sell without a considerable loss—just as I can't sell without a greater loss. He undertook to borrow money from Mr. Steiner. He wanted to do it without disturbing his credit relations. I mean, he did not want, for professional reasons, to put up any of his own collateral."

Bull looked curiously at her.

"Didn't you tell me you knew nothing about your husband's business affairs?"

"No. I didn't. I told you once that my husband never discussed his affairs with me."

It was Bull's turn to be surprised. Before he could ask more the bell rang, and the maid announced Dr. Bellamy. Bull looked covertly at his watch. It was past ten o'clock. An odd time for even an old friend of the family to call. Mrs. Colton hesitated, and he rose.

"If you'll excuse me, I'll be getting along. I'll see you in the morning."

Then Mrs. Colton did a very surprising thing. She held out her hand impulsively. Bull took it clumsily. She smiled a bright wistful little smile.

"I'm sorry about all this. But . . . well, I'll see you in the morning."

Bull met Dr. Bellamy in the hall. They nodded to each other. Bull went out quickly. He had one more thing to do, before he reached out the long arm of the law. Was it for Albert Steiner? Doaks? Michael Royce? Inspector Bull did not know.

CHAPTER TWENTY-NINE

Bull left the underground at Chancery-lane and started around the corner. Near the entrance to the station he came upon an old crone trying to sell a bunch of soiled violets to a very much intoxicated young man in evening clothes.

The young man, propped perilously against the wall, was making superhuman efforts to get some pennies out of his trousers pocket. The old woman was giving him as much help as she thought would escape the eye of any passing constable. The young man was saying, "Don't cry, little flower girl."

Bull hesitated, trying to decide whether he was justified as a member of the C.I.D. to stop the old woman, or as a fellow being to help the young man, when the flower seller's voice made him stop short and step back out of the light.

"Orl right, sir, tyke these 'ere lahvely posies 'ome to your lidy."

She whined ingratiatingly, and made a sudden dive for a half crown that rolled out of the young man's pocket. She retrieved it, looked at it, thrust it into the ragged folds of a voluminous filthy cloak and made off down Holborn, leaving the dilapidated bunch of violets on the pavement in front of her client.

Another coincidence in the same spot was more than the most inveterate gambler—which Bull was not—could have anticipated. That the old woman whom he and Royce had met coming out of the mortuary, where she had been to identify Gates, should be in almost the exact spot where

Peskett and Doaks had their rendezvous, was much too significant to pass over. Bull took a last appraising glance at the young man, who was making a futile effort to pick up the violets, and set out discreetly after the woman.

Without a glance either way she turned, with surprising agility, it seemed to Bull, into the narrow passage leading from Holborn to the gates of Gray's Inn. Bull followed. She was peering through the closed gates. Bull could hear her whine as she spoke to the porter, but he could not hear what she was saying. After a few moments she turned and went back to Holborn, passing Bull without a glance. He went up quickly to the porter.

"I'm Inspector Bull, Scotland Yard," he said urgently. "What did the old woman want?"

The porter shook his head.

"Balmy, sir," he said. "As near as I could make out it was Mr. Field's man Doaks as she wanted. I sent her around the other way, and I told her she'd better be minding her own affairs."

Bull thanked him and went back to Holborn and west to the passage leading to Jockey's-fields. The old woman—who he hadn't the least doubt was Constable Porter's Lizzie, shuffled easily along with no attempt at concealment. She was peering up at the names in the registers. When she came to No. 8-A she stopped, looked up and down, and went across to the other side of the road. Inspector Bull sauntered leisurely into the street. She sank down in a door-way, one eye on Bull, the other on Mr. Field's dining room window, and pretended to sleep. She was absolutely still. Once she raised her head; she had seen a white glass-curtain move as if somebody had brushed against it. Bull came almost even with her and threw her a few coppers.

"Gawd bless you, sir," she mumbled. Bull passed on.

In Mr. Field's dining room a man stood discreetly concealed from the outside by the long maroon velvet window hangings. Now and then he drew the glass-curtains aside and gazed intently down into the dimly lighted road. He saw an old woman come along from the Holborn end and disappear. Then he saw her cross the road directly beneath him. She glanced up at the window where he stood and sank down in a doorway. The man looked down at her with a puzzled air. He would have thought she was just a homeless old hag sleeping in any open doorway, but he knew the London nomads. A certain instinct drew them to the same hole every night. She had never been there before. She must have some

130

purpose; and the man dreaded anyone watching that house with a purpose.

He fingered the revolver in his hands, which trembled less now than when he had taken it—three shells missing—from his box upstairs a few minutes before.

He saw a very large man come slowly down the road, toss the old woman some coins. He saw her quick movement to get them. He recognised Inspector Bull, and moved forward, drawing the curtains a little to the left with his free hand. Not a movement, not a sound, warned him that he was not alone; then a grip as strong as a vise paralysed his hand. The gun slipped to the floor. Without releasing his hold John Field stooped and picked it up. He turned it over in his hand, examining it thoughtfully.

"That's enough of that, Doaks," he said quietly, and put the revolver in his pocket.

Bull hailed a taxi in Theobald's-road and went to the Ship to meet Walters. He was so late that Walters had nearly given him up.

"Sorry," Bull said. "I'll see if I can't show you something tonight."

He excused himself, found a telephone, and gave rapid orders to Scotland Yard. A constable in uniform was to parade around Gray's Inn and disturb the old woman across from 8-A, Jockey's-fields without alarming her. He wanted to get her back to her stand at St. Andrew's in Upper Thames-street. Bull thought a while. Then he ordered the removal of the operative watching the Colton household, and directed him to be stationed in a shop across St. Giles-street from the jeweller's. He was to make no effort to stop anyone from going in.

The great bell of St. Paul's was just striking midnight when the two came in sight of the grey tower of the deserted St. Andrew's. The constable in uniform had done his duty; Bull reached down and prodded the snoring bundle of filth and rags crouched in the corner against the ancient grey wall. Lizzie stirred. They heard a few Thames-side imprecations. She struggled to her feet and glowered sullenly at the men in front of her. Then she recognised Bull; he knew it by the crafty light that glinted an instant in her bleary faded eyes, and the ingratiating smirk on her drunken face.

Another change came over her that Bull did not miss either. At first she remembered him as the man who had given her coppers; then the dark shadow of fear passed behind the

131

watery eyes. She cringed, wiping her mouth with the back of a grimy hand. She had put two and two together with the quickness of the street-tramp, and they had worked out at "Police."

"Look here, mother," Bull said. "I want to know what happened here last night."

She blinked cunningly at him.

"Out with it, now. I want to know all about it. I saw you coming out of the mortuary. You went there to see the man who was drowned at the bottom of the lane down there. And what were you doing at Gray's Inn?"

Bull knew that with this wretched creature it was simply a question of where the most profit would come. She gave him a calculating glance; he knew now that she did know something for him.

" 'Ow much do I get?" she said simply.

In ten minutes Bull had his story, which was exactly what he expected. Stripped of its flavour and ramblings into her own life-history and the grievances of her class, it was simple.

Paul's had struck one when two men came along. It was very dark. She thought one was blind, because the other was leading him. They did not know the locality well, or they would have known she was there. She was always there. And she had been sleeping by St. Andrew's long enough to know that men didn't come to Upper Thames-street, especially turning down Trig-lane, at one o'clock, for any good purposes. She was afraid to follow down towards the river, but she kept her eyes open. They turned down the lane. She thought of calling the constable (that Bull doubted). She changed her mind. In three or four minutes, one man came back up the lane. He was of medium height, slightly stooped, and in a hurry. Lizzie stayed in her corner until he was out of sight; she couldn't keep up with him, but she figured that he might either go across the Bridge, or over Blackfriars westward, or up to Ludgate-circus. In the latter case she could get there ahead of him, if he went, as he looked to be doing, the longest way. Her shrewdness was repaid. She went as fast as she could to Fleet-street. The man came rapidly up from Ludgate-circus, turned up Chancery-lane and went into Gray's Inn. She saw him twice under a light; he wore a grey soft hat and a funny brown coat—funny because the sleeves were too short.

Bull nodded. He had seen the same coat.

After that Lizzie came back to St. Andrew's and went down Trig-lane to investigate. She saw nothing except a hat crushed against the wall. In the morning, before her trip to the mortuary, she went back to Holborn in hopes of seeing her man. She did not see him. She went back again afterwards late in the afternoon, and coming up towards the Inn at the bottom of Bedford-row had had the great fortune to meet him. She followed him discreetly; he went to market in Lamb's Conduit-street; and she watched him enter No. 8-A in Jockey's-fields when he had finished.

That was that. Bull and his companion went in silence to Ludgate-circus.

"I want to think a moment," Bull said.

Laboriously he brought the whole box of pieces of his jig-saw puzzle out and looked them over.

Michael and Agatha Colton quarrelling and packing for France because each was too proud to say, "I'm sorry, I didn't really mean it."

Michael and his mother quarrelling, and Michael burning the letter Gates had written.

Mrs. Royce and the £500 cheque for Mrs. Colton.

Mrs. Colton being short of ready cash.

Mr. Colton being short of ready cash, and trying to get the money from Steiner.

Steiner's departure for Brussels.

His talk with Mrs. Colton the night before he had gone.

The visit of Dr. Bellamy at ten o'clock that evening.

Field's chance remark about Colton's jealousy of the doctor.

Doaks—and the money he was getting from somewhere.

Peskett—and the money he had got from somewhere.

Gates. Gates's death. Gates walking like a blind man; Doaks leading him confidently. Bull reflected here that not many people knew Trig-lane and the death steps leading down into the Thames—only people who had been brought up on London streets.

Doaks lived in Slough. Sough was near both Windsor and Colnbrook.

And that brought him back to the £500 cheque, and to Mrs. Colton, and to the death of Oliver Peskett.

Bull stopped short. He remembered that there had been a fine film of powder on the bolt he had found in Agatha Colton's powder table.

The idea of the eternal triangle had never been very far from Bull's mind since he had first seen Louise Colton. She was beautiful; there was no doubt that she was unhappy. Her husband was not admirable where his women were concerned. And in Bull's mind he had arranged and re-arranged the points of the triangle. None of them fitted. He had thought of

133

the solicitor; he had abandoned that idea after the visit to his chambers. He had thought of young Royce until he saw him with Agatha at the Corner House. He was ashamed to admit that he had even thought of Peskett, until Peskett had been killed. But he had never once thought of Albert Steiner —not even when Mrs. Colton had told him she had learned the details of her husband's business from the jeweller in Hatton-garden. Inspector Bull was Nordic to the core.

And then, in a flash, it came to Bull, and he knew at least a part of what had happened—and who had done it. Gates, he said to himself, Gates. There was the key. Gates was the mystery man of the piece. No one knew him, where he came from, what he had done, why he had been killed. The only facts about him were that in life he had worked for Colton, in death he lay now covered with a sheet in the mortuary.

Bull hailed a taxi.

"St. Giles-street, Bond-street," he said. "Come along, Walters. I think you're going to get your story."

Then he lapsed into silence. Walters had a good reportorial indifference; also he knew how to wait.

Bull continued to think it over. The empty satchel at Trig-lane bottom, the humble report of the constable on duty at St. Giles-street. Gates had gone to Colton's locked shop and had tried to get in. When the constable appeared he had got the wind up. He had gone to keep his engagement at Upper Thames-street, but he had gone empty-handed; Bull knew now that he had never had the jewels—and that the black satchel had long been empty. That was another blind, and a shrewd one. That was intended to mislead him, and had very nearly done so. The blow that killed Gates was not struck to get the diamonds. It was struck to remove Gates.

At the top of St. Giles-street Bull stopped the taxi. They got out. Bull waited until the taxi had disappeared in the darkness.

"This way," Bull said quietly. He set off down the dark old street. He glanced up at the shop across from Colton's. There was no sign of life in it. Bull nodded approvingly.

"No noise!" he said in a whisper to Walters, who nodded.

Bull took the keys from his pocket and unlocked the heavily shuttered shop. They stepped inside; Bull quietly closed the door and locked it again.

The shop was as dark as pitch.

"Look out for the cat," Bull whispered, before he remembered that Mrs. Colton had taken the cat to Cadogan-square.

He took out his pocket flash and rapidly surveyed the room

in the circle of yellow light. Nothing had been disturbed since the morning he and Mr. Field had inspected the place. There had been no liquidation of the stock. Centuries of silence brooded over the low-ceilinged room.

"This way," Bull whispered, and led the way into the back room. Again the yellow circle of light played quickly around the room. They came back into the main room of the shop. The flash rested for an instant on the open cupboard door.

"Get in there," Bull whispered. "Stay there. If you make a noise I'll shoot you myself."

"Right you are, old fellow," Walters said quietly. He entered the cupboard philosophically.

"Cigarettes allowed?" he whispered.

Bull snarled under his breath.

"Not a sound," he repeated.

Again the darting circle. Bull moved towards the steps and went stealthily up them. The room was black again.

CHAPTER THIRTY

Walters waited silently. Above he could hear the faint tread of Inspector Bull, very faint through the solid oak floor. Then the creaking of the stairs. There was no light.

"All right," Bull whispered. "Stay there no matter what happens. Keep still!"

The shop was as silent as the grave. They waited. Somewhere in the distance a clock struck two. Walters shifted his weight uneasily. There was a warning hiss from the darkness. Where Bull was he did not know. Gradually Walters lost all feeling except for the throb, throb, throb of his own heart. His eyes became used to the darkness; he could make out the outlines of a coat hanging in the cupboard.

Then outside, in the street, he heard a faint sound. Was it a stealthy footfall? A second later there was a faint noise inside the room. Then the faintest rasp of metal. Then a sound that Walters was certain of; the click of a turning lock.

Walters moved closer to the wall behind the cupboard door. He heard the shop door open, saw a faint shaft of light; it came over the cupboard door and passed rapidly along. He heard the door close almost noiselessly. Then silence again.

Walters strained his ears. There was no sound. The thought came to him that Bull had gone out; a cold sweat broke out on him; he could feel the quicker beat of his heart. He was about to move when he felt something near him. He was not touched, he simply knew that someone was in the room, moving towards him. He downed the mad impulse to spring out shouting. He stood almost breathless, trying to quiet the beat of his heart, unconscious of his clenched fists.

Then he saw a faint light. Someone besides Bull was using a torch. Then the faintest creaking of the stairs. The light was on steadily. It was growing dimmer; it disappeared. Still no sound. A moment lengthening into a century passed. No light, no sound. Then the creaking of the stairs again; the light, dim, increasing. Then utter darkness. Again he felt the movement towards him. Again he strained every nerve to keep silent.

There was a sudden rush of feet, a startled cry, an oath.

"Lights!" Bull shouted. "By the door!"

Walters leaped out of the cupboard into the dark, stumbled drunk with excitement across blindly towards the door, fumbled for the switch. Fumbled interminably, while the gasping, the oaths and the struggling went on. Found the switch. The room was flooded with almost blinding light.

Inspector Bull was sitting on a man in the middle of the floor, his great hands holding the man's hands down on the carpet.

"Take the gun out of his hip pocket," he said breathlessly. "See the brown coat with short sleeves?"

Walters took out the revolver and Bull got up.

"All right, Mr. Field," he said.

Murder blazed in Field's blue eyes, burning dangerously in his ashen face. He got up. His gaze followed Bull's to the green baize bag on the floor. His breath came quickly. His eyes shifted back to the gleaming blue steel in Bull's hand, darted towards the door.

"Pick up that bag," Bull said. "Put it on the table. Telephone Scotland Yard. Then go across the street and shout to my man in the haberdasher's."

He looked steadily at John Field. A shudder ran through Field.

"May I ask what I'm charged with?" he said, in a voice quivering and twisted with passion. "I suppose you know I haven't broken in here. I have Mrs. Colton's keys."

"You are not charged with burglary, Mr. Field," Bull said slowly. "I want you for the murder of George Colton and of James B. Gates. And I warn you that anything you say may be used against you. And—speaking unofficially—allow me to compliment you. It was clever work."

Field smiled unpleasantly.

"Thank you, Inspector. What about Peskett? Aren't you forgetting something?"

"I'm not forgetting anything," Bull said as coolly. "You killed Colton and Gates. You did not kill Peskett."

Field bowed.

"Thanks so much. May I sit down?"

Bull nodded. His eyes were steadily on Field, the revolver in his hand never wavered.

Field had recovered his self-possession.

"May I smoke, Inspector?"

"Certainly."

In the door came Walters, and with him a short stocky man with a stolid face and keen eyes. He saluted, and looked at Field with a pleased smile.

Bull handed him the revolver.

"Be careful with that man," he said placidly. "He's dangerous."

Field smiled again. Bull stood looking at him. He felt that something was still wrong; and he knew that when he had such a feeling something was wrong. He watched Field intently. The solicitor was perfectly willing to sit there. More; he wanted to sit there.

Bull glanced at the green bag on the table. He did not move from in front of the door.

"Hand me that bag, Walters," he said.

He opened it and looked inside. He glanced over at Field. Field nodded.

"That's the diamonds, all right. Gates returned them to me last night. I'm taking them to Mrs. Royce. Perhaps you already guessed as much."

Bull smiled and handed the bag to Walters. As he did so he caught a quick movement from Field. There was no sign from Bull; but he had seen the solicitor quickly push back his cuff and look at his watch.

Bull thought. That was it; playing for time. Why? It was nearly three. Suddenly Bull understood. He went quickly into the back room and took up the telephone. After a time that seemed endless he got the Colton house. A sleepy voice answered.

"Mrs. Colton, please."

"I'm sorry, she's gone abroad."

"Who's speaking? This is Inspector Bull."

"It's Mrs. Coggins, sir."

"Where's the new maid?"

137

"Sacked, sir, this very night."

Bull rang off. He blew his nose violently in deep thought and went back to the front room.

"By the way, Mr. Field," he said, "what did you do with your servant?"

"Doaks?" said Field calmly. He hesitated a moment, then shrugged his shoulders.

"Oh, well, Inspector, I suppose it's all up. You have the better of me. You'll find him in the second floor closet."

"Dead?"

"Oh, no. Tied up."

Bull nodded.

"It doesn't make much difference to you which it was, does it?"

"Not very much, Inspector," Mr. Field said with a smile.

There was a knocking at the door. Two men came in.

"Take this man to the Yard," Bull said. "Hold him. You go out to 8-A Jockey's-fields, Gray's Inn, and get the valet, Doaks. Tied up in a closet on the second floor."

The telephone rang.

"Hello, Bull speaking. What? Where? Well, I'm damned."

Scotland Yard reported an urgent call from Mr. Pinkerton to Bull. He was on Wimbledon Common. It was urgent.

For a moment Bull was speechless with wrath. Pinkerton could go to the devil; the further from London the little Welshman was the better pleased Bull would be. Then he thought about it. If Pinkerton sent such a message it meant something. There was no telling what had happened to him. Once Bull had got him out of jail, once he had got him out of a house just before a box of dynamite had exploded in the cellar. Each time Mr. Pinkerton had been doing something.

Bull stepped out into the street. A long low car was waiting.

"The Commissioner said you'd need this, sir," the driver said.

"Thanks," Bull said. He got in. Walters calmly got in too. "We're going to Wimbledon Common. I don't know whereabouts on it."

"I do, sir. The Chief gave me the directions himself."

Bull grunted. The car tore through Knightsbridge, Sloane-street, King's-road, across Putney-bridge, out Merton-road, out to the edge of the Common, and turned in Coombe-lane. The car came to a stop.

"That'll be them!" the driver said. He pointed to a car a hundred yards off across the Common. Bull jumped out and ran across the grass. A little figure dashed frantically to meet him.

"Pinkerton!" Bull cried. "What in Heaven's name . . ."

"This way! this way!" the little man gasped. He turned and fled back the way he had come. Bull followed.

Pinkerton stopped at the motor-car. Bull recognised it; it was the Coltons' Daimler. In it Mrs. Colton lay unconscious. Fifty feet away, engine running quietly, stood a monoplane. It was ready for flight.

Bull took it all in dumbly. His gaze went back to the beautiful face, so pale against the dark cushions. Pinkerton jerked urgently at his sleeve. Bull turned to see still another car drive rapidly up. It came to a stop. A man jumped out, carrying a small satchel, and ran towards them. Bull recognised him; it was Dr. Bellamy. Without a word the doctor pushed him aside and opened the door of the car. He raised Mrs. Colton in his arms and rolled her eye-lids back from her eyes.

Bull shuddered. She was dead. Perhaps it was the best way. Pinkerton jerked again at his sleeve. Bull shook him off.

"Let's see if she's still alive first," he said.

Mr. Pinkerton almost screamed. "She's not dead," he shouted. "She's drugged, you ass."

Bull stared at him.

"For mercy's sake," cried Mr. Pinkerton, as near profanity as he ever came, "*will* you come on and quit staring like a great ox?"

Bull turned to him in astonishment.

"This way! This way!"

He ran towards the monoplane.

"She's over here, I've got her. There, in the cockpit!"

Bull came heavily up, and looked in the cockpit. Agatha Colton was bound hand and foot with long strips of her own silk lingerie. An open suitcase on the grass showed where Mr. Pinkerton had taken his improvised bonds. Bull looked at her. The dark eyes stared at him with blazing hatred, terrible, implacable.

"She murdered Peskett," Mr. Pinkerton said breathlessly. "She drugged Mrs. Colton. She would have murdered her if it hadn't been for Bellamy. Her lover killed her father and Gates."

"Michael Royce?" said Bull.

"No. Field, John Field."

Bull took off his hat. There was still no word from Agatha Colton. Bull looked sharply at her. She had slumped down in the corner. A small phial slipped out of the lifeless hand she had managed to free before it was too late.

139

CHAPTER THIRTY-ONE

Two days later Inspector Bull knocked on the Commissioner's door.

"Hello, Bull. Good work. Sit down."

"Thank you, sir," Bull said. "It wasn't really me. Field was easy. It was the girl that was hard. I'd never have guessed it in the world."

Debenham grinned and pushed over his box of cigars.

"You see, sir, when I found the bolt in her powder table, I was sure Mrs. Colton had planted it there. I never thought of the girl's planting it on herself. Pinkerton thinks she didn't plant it—she didn't know I'd seen it on Peskett's door, and never thought I'd look for it. He's probably right. When I did find it she was intelligent enough to let it go. Not many women are that intelligent."

"Nor men either, Bull; be fair."

"So I got started wrong, sir. I thought Mrs. Colton had fired those two shots that night on the Colnbrook Road. I didn't think she'd shoot as wild as all that unless she meant to. She nearly hit the driver, so when he was shot I said to myself, 'She's done it right this time.' She says now she wasn't trying to hit the man, just frighten him."

"I see, Bull. But I take it Field wasn't frightened into shooting Colton?"

"Not him, sir. It was all planned. It was the girl, really. She was a vicious one. She hated Louise Colton, and she hated her father for marrying her. She tried to get away, but her father wouldn't let her go. So she took matters into her own hands."

"Through Field?"

"Well, Field was in love with her. He put all his money into her account at Lloyd's in Paris if anything happened to him; and he tried to hold me until she got away. Then there was the money."

"She had a fair income, didn't she?"

"As it turned out, she did, sir. But there was the rub. Colton was hard up. He'd tied everything up so his wife couldn't get it until some time after he'd died. Then he found he needed cash, so he started converting the securities he'd left his daughter. They were the easiest negotiated. Field protested; the old fellow swore he'd cut the girl off without a shilling. I don't doubt he would have done, too. So they decided to put an end to it. It was the girl who persuaded him to come back by Colnbrook. Field told me this. She asked her father to pick her up at the Lane-Frazier's on the Road; said she was having dinner there. He didn't like to explain his reasons to people."

"And young Royce?"

"Well, the girl was entirely unscrupulous, sir. His mother kept telling him she didn't really care for him at all. That's what they quarrelled about. Then Gates wrote Mrs. Royce a letter saying Agatha and Field had been negotiating for the sale of diamonds with an underground buyer in Antwerp. She told her son that. He raised a terrible row and was off to France. When he heard Peskett was killed he knew Agatha had done it and decided to stand by. She wasn't waiting for a call from him. She was just pretending, getting a good pettish reason for going off to Paris.

"You see, it started—or the complications did—when Peskett recognised Field. He started to blackmail him. He got hold of Doaks and paid him to let him into Field's rooms. He was looking for the revolver and also for the diamonds. Field, after he'd shot Colton, drove to Cranford, got his car out of an empty estate garden and came calmly in to town. He unlocked the shop—with keys he'd got from Colton— and simply put the diamonds in the top drawer of Colton's private desk. I was fooled by the gold key. I almost had my hands on them the first time I went in the place."

"It was Field who was there that night?"

Bull nodded.

"Not Gates?"

"Gates was never near the place, after the murder. He was on a buying trip. And that's a funny thing, sir."

Debenham looked up from the squares and circles he was drawing on his desk pad.

"What is?"

"That trip. Do you remember the emerald collar that belonged to the Dowager?"

Debenham grinned.

"Rather."

"Well, you see Steiner is mad about diamonds. Colton wasn't. But as Steiner told me—and I should have known he had a reason—Colton would sell his soul for emeralds. Gates was in Nice, negotiating with Lady Blanche for her mother-in-law's emeralds. Gates got them for Colton for £15,000 cash."

"Is that where the emeralds were lost?" Debenham said

with a grin. "Good Lord! Dryden persuaded me an American gang had got them; he sailed yesterday for New York and Chicago."

Bull allowed himself a respectful smile.

"Well, sir, I think Gates got the £15,000 on the promise of Mrs. Royce's diamonds; and I *think* it was from Steiner. The whole thing of course was grossly illegal. That's why Gates got the wind up and had to lie low. He had the emeralds and not only that, he had already taken them out of the Duchess's collar. He put them in a deposit vault in Brussels and came back to tell Mrs. Colton, Mrs. Royce and Field the whole story. By that time the police were after him and he lost his head. Then he found out that somebody was negotiating with the Belgian fence Arnaud, and that it was Field. He got in touch with Field. This comes from a letter I got this morning from Steiner, and from Field. Well, then Field was going to turn the diamonds over to him to take to Mrs. Royce. Gates knew Hammersmith, Shepherd's Bush and Bond-street; he didn't know Trig-lane.

"In the meantime when Field saw I was on Doaks's track he planted his gun in Doaks's box and wore Doaks's overcoat. All he had to do to get rid of Doaks was to leave the brandy out. And Doaks found the gun in his box, and was on the point of signalling me when Field caught him and tied him up."

Debenham smiled.

"Jackson pulled Doaks out of the linen press that night," he said. "Field had done a good job of tying up. Much better, I judge, than Pinkerton did with Miss Colton's chemises, or whatever they call them nowadays."

"He was lucky Field rather liked him," Bull commented.

"Precisely. You haven't told me how Mr. Pinkerton discovered Agatha."

"He says he knew it was Agatha as soon as I found the bolt in her table, and she mentioned how soundly she'd slept. I don't believe it. I think he was still following Mrs. Colton. He was sure at first that she was in it. I think he sort of happened on to Agatha."

Bull's sober face became more sober as he thought of Mrs. Colton.

"You see, Mrs. Colton was sure she was being drugged, but she was afraid to say so. She called Bellamy. He refused to let her stay in the house alone. She used to smuggle him in after Agatha was out of the way. Agatha knew it, and she and Field decided to polish her off. In that case Agatha would get the whole fortune. She drugged Mrs. Colton's coffee with Luminall and got her into the car. I don't think she would have been found, out there on the Common, for a long time. Agatha hated her like poison. Well, Pinkerton was watching; he saw them come out, and he hung onto the spare tire. Out on the Common he had quite a tussle with Agatha. I should have thought she was stronger than he was. Then he found a man to take the telephone message."

Bull smiled. So did the Commissioner.

"It was the fastest ride he ever had."

"Well, Bull, what *was* the little gold key?"

Bull blushed.

"It was the key to his first wife's jewel box. It was to go to Agatha at her marriage."

"You got off on Mrs. Royce too, Bull, I think." The Commissioner smiled again. "When you've known as many old Tartars of the late reign as I have, Bull, you'll never suspect them of anything more than a desire to be loyal, kind and generous without anybody's knowing it."

There was a knock on the door.

"Mr. Steiner to see you, sir."

"Ask him to come in. Hello, Mr. Steiner. You know Inspector Bull."

"Very well," said Albert Steiner. He peered myopically at Bull, and smiled his dark enigmatic smile.

"Why did you go, Mr. Steiner?" Bull asked. "Do you mind telling me?"

"I will gladly tell you. I went because you were going to arrest me, and Mr. Field was going to shoot me; and I was afraid Mr. Field would be first. I was trying to tell you what it was all about, Inspector, when I told you that Colton was fond of emeralds. I've known Mr. Field for many years. I've warned Mrs. Colton as much as I dared. I'm very glad she is free. She is a beautiful woman. One of the few women I've known who can really wear diamonds."

In Cadogan-square Louise Colton, Dr. Bellamy and Mr. Pinkerton were having tea.

"I don't know how I can ever thank you, Mr. Pinkerton," she said. Her eyes still bore traces of the harrowing three weeks.

"You mustn't try, ma'am," Mr. Pinkerton stammered, blushing behind the steel-rimmed spectacles. "You see, I knew about Dr. Bellamy. I knew he would want to know, because when I first began to watch your house, he used to walk by. In fact, we each suspected the other for a while— until I saw his face one night when he looked up at your window."

Dr. Bellamy flushed like a school-boy. Louise Colton smiled charmingly.

"If you'll excuse me, I think I shall go to Scotland Yard to find my friend Inspector Bull."

Mr. Pinkerton long considered that his most tactful remark. He got his hat and let himself out of the front door.

"You ought to get away from here, Louise," Dr. Bellamy said gruffly. "You look perfectly ghastly."

"I know," she said, wistfully gazing out of the window. "But I hate to go alone."

"I'll wire your brother. He can take you to Italy or Norway or somewhere."

She shook her lovely pale gold head.

"What about Mrs. Royce, then?"

"Or one of the lions in Trafalgar-square."

He shrugged his shoulders.

The corners of her mouth slowly began to quiver, and her eyes filled with tears.

"I can't think of anyone else," he said helplessly, and looked at her.

Louise Colton was crying.

Bellamy was on his knees beside her. She was sobbing like a tired child in his arms. He didn't feel helpless any longer. The years he had adored her and been afraid of her, watched her growing up, marrying George Colton, had thought he hated her for it, were gone. She was his. Her sobs gradually became quieter, then stopped. She looked up, and the grief had gone from her eyes.

"Darling," she whispered, "don't make me go away! Please!"